Christmas in April

Olivia Almagro

ISBN: 979-8-9989067-0-1

K.A.M.'s Publishing

Los Angeles, CA 90008

www.kimamorrow.com

Dedication

I offer this book as a loving dedication to you,
my parents, Charles A. Brown and Alicia Almagro,
whose guidance and grace shaped my life.

Table of Contents

Acknowledgements:

First, I thank God for His unconditional love. I praise You every waking moment.

To my parents, Charles A. Brown and Alicia Almagro: This book is for you. I thank God for the blessing of being born to you and for the life you gave me.

To my oldest sister, Alicia Zayas, the matriarch of our family—I love you.

To my brother, John Almagro: Thank you for always being there for me and believing in me. You are truly an older brother. You laugh at all my corny jokes, and I don't know what I would do without you. Love you!

To my brother, Robert Almagro Sr., who reminds me so much of our father—I love you dearly.

To my best friends, Kimberly A. Morrow and Dr. Stacie A. Morris: Your friendship means the world to me. I am so blessed to journey through life with you. Love you always.

Chanel Taylor—my sister from another mother. Thank you for your constant support and encouragement. I deeply value our friendship.

Eva Jane Bunkley—my sister-friend. I am proud of you and grateful for all the years you have stood by me. I love you.

Anna Mariotti—thank you for your friendship. It means so much to me. A spa date is long overdue. Love you!

To my cousin, Caroline Brown in the UK: I adore you and love you. This life journey has been so much sweeter with you in it. Love you!

Karen McLean—thank you for always being there and for writing the foreword for *Christmas in April*. I appreciate you.

Cecilia Campillo – *Mi querida prima, gracias por todo. Aprecio tu apoyo. Te quiero mucho.*

Francis Hernandez—Thank you, my friend, for supporting my literary journey. I appreciate your feedback.

Yvonne R. Davis - So happy we are back to being friends. So thankful for our friendship.

To my childhood friend Tiffany: I love you, and I am grateful for your constant presence in my life. From second grade to now—what a blessing. Thank you for being a friend. Traveled down the road and back again. 🎵🎵

To my childhood friend Kenny Freeman. I truly appreciate our friendship and the many adventures we have shared, especially our journeys through the virtual streets of the Worlds.

To my childhood friend and sister, Verlecuia "Lisa" Mitchell: Thank you for your support. Love you dearly.

Yasmín S. Portales-Machado - Thank you for your invaluable support in helping me ensure the historical facts are accurate.

Larry McColley—my fellow Brownite and brother. I appreciate you and value our friendship. Love you.

Dr. Edmund H. Moore—thank you for your wisdom and steadfast support. I consider it a blessing to know you.

To my editor, Gina Casto: Thank you for your invaluable support. I truly appreciate you and all that you do.

Foreword

I have known Olivia Almagro for as long as I can remember, since we were babies. As children of immigrant parents, we grew up with an understanding of the sacrifices, expectations, and dreams carried by those who left everything behind to build a better life. Arriving in a new land, where there's an unfamiliarity in language, culture, work, and politics, can be daunting, especially when tasked with raising bright-eyed, first-generation children.

My earliest memories with Olivia include stories from her mother about the mystique of Cuba, tales of perseverance at Sunday dinners filled with roast pork, *frijoles negros* and *arroz*, and the love of family. It's this rich cultural tapestry that shines through in Olivia's writing. I've watched her grow into a gifted storyteller, capturing fast-paced drama, a tender romance, and, in this book, the unpredictable journey of a family bound by love, courage, and grace as they chase the American dream.

As a seasoned social worker with over thirty years of experience that also included serving immigrant families, *Christmas in April* resonated with me. I've heard countless stories from newly arrived families grappling with fear, uncertainty, and the feeling of leaving behind everything while clinging to the hope they made the right choice. It takes courage to leave, faith to stay the course, and resilience to build something new from nothing. Family support is a privilege not every immigrant has. Yet for the Martinez family, the principle of *"somos familia"*—we are family, and "family always has your back" is the thread that holds everything together.

Their journey from Cuba to Paterson, New Jersey, was fueled by sheer determination and belief in the promise of a better life. In *Christmas in April*, we meet Guillermo and Rosa, a Cuban couple who arrive in the U.S. with little more than hope in their eyes and dreams in their hearts. Paterson becomes the backdrop for their transformation as they face language barriers, moments of despair, and eventually, triumph.

Though the characters are immigrants, their story is universal at best. As Guillermo confronts personal struggles that threaten the family's foundation, Rosa discovers a powerful voice and strength she never knew she had. Their three children, one born in the U.S., navigate the space between cultures, excelling in school, making friends, and ultimately becoming the family's compass in this unfamiliar land. Their adaptability becomes a beacon of hope, reminding us that while the American dream isn't easy, it's still attainable through unity and perseverance.

This is a story of love, loss, transformation, and survival. It reminds us that every immigrant carries not only a past, but a future waiting to unfold. The family on these pages may be fictional, or they may be your neighbors, your coworkers, or even a reflection of your own family. Either way, their story will resonate. Their strength will inspire.

Welcome to their journey.

Dr. Karen McLean, PhD, MSW

Author's Note

Penning *Christmas in April* was one of the most personal things I have done. I was born and raised in Hartford, Connecticut, to an Afro-Cuban mom and Jamaican dad, who taught me what life is about, what values to live by, and their amazing power to endure and thrive.

Even though this novel is fiction, it is built on the genuine experiences of migration, and the ability to do something as daring and brave as giving up everything you know. It is also a story about the consequences that often come with such actions, and the bravery to start a life not only for oneself, but also for their children.

The family at the core of this story lives through multiple identities, not just as a Cuban family, but as Afro-Cubans facing the realities of being racially Black in America.

This book is inspired by the Rositas of the world, women like my mom and like the families who left behind everything they knew, only to face new challenges on the other side of freedom. And still, they carried themselves with dignity as they began anew.

Christmas in April was shaped by kitchen-table conversations, barbershop talk, and the dreams that once felt deferred. While Rosa and Guillermo are fictional, their struggles, sacrifices, and love for their children are deeply real to me and, I imagine, to many of you.

I thought it was befitting to name each chapter after a Celia Cruz song, a small offering of gratitude to my roots and a salute to the Queen of Salsa. In celebration of her centennial, her music serves as both the cultural heartbeat and emotional backdrop of the story, infusing every page with the rhythm, resilience, and spirit that have long defined the Cuban people.

This book is my tribute to the mothers and fathers who carried their children across oceans of hardship, traveled unfamiliar terrain, and to the children who grew up straddling two cultures, trying to make sense of both.

I want to thank you for reading this story. I hope you see your own family reflected in these pages. And I hope *Christmas in April* reminds you that even in the most unexpected seasons, joy, healing, and new beginnings can still take root and flourish.

With love and gratitude,

Olivia Almagro

Chapter 1

La Vida Es un Carnaval

I had finally dozed off just as my husband, Guillermo, stumbled home in the wee hours of the morning. The roosters that roamed freely in our yard sounded the alarm, squawking and flapping their wings as if they too disapproved of him returning at such an ungodly hour. He fumbled with the latch on the front gate, the same gate his father welded by hand, the creak of the front door adding to the morning stillness. The house we built together, brick by brick, sweat in every corner. The house we were to leave behind for a better life in America.

The smell of rum and tobacco leached from his skin, thick and sour, like a magnetic force that knew no bounds. It entered the room before he did, weaving through the mosquito netting and sinking into the curtains. But something else followed. The unmistakable scent of another woman's perfume.

Her sour bodily fluid mingled with salt and sweat had gripped to his clothes like a second skin. I recognized it, though I pretended not to. Those days of questioning his whereabouts and fighting with other women in the streets over him were over. My pride wouldn't allow it, so I simply pretended the other women didn't exist.

Inside, my heart had been shattered. I was devastated and broken by a series of betrayals that could have destroyed me, had I not faced the truth: Guillermo wasn't just my husband, he was my first love. The only man I had ever loved: *el papá de mis hijos.*

The problem was that we married so young. We thought borrowed rings and a baby meant forever. So I stopped asking where he'd been, partly because I was afraid I'd lose him. Besides, it was just too painful to have the truth spoken aloud.

There were days I had no *energia* to get out of bed, but I did it for my family. I was determined that our family would stay together no matter what came our way. I didn't fight to bring these children into this world to raise them by myself. So, I stopped checking pockets and sniffing his clothes while I hand washed them on a makeshift wooden baseboard outside and hung his clothes out to dry. What was the point? The truth always found a way to crawl home anyway on his breath and under his fingernails.

Still, I kept washing his clothes. I kept laying out his plate. I kept sleeping on my side of the bed like a good wife, because in our world, leaving your husband meant you'd failed. And I hadn't failed at anything in my life except maybe choosing who I believed to be the right man. I wanted Guillermo because at the time, I didn't know I had the right to want better. Like most nights, I kept my eyes closed, breathing slow and steady, the rhythm of sleep faked to perfection. His drunken body bumped into the table, then the dresser, as he yanked off his trousers and the button-down shirt I had gifted him for his birthday. He cursed under his breath, "*singao*," frustrated with the buttons, frustrated with himself, frustrated with me, I imagined. He fell into bed beside me and began snoring almost at once, his head tilted upright, mouth open, breath heavy with rum.

While I lay there, my mind churned with the weight of leaving the only place we had ever known and stepping into a beginning that felt more like exile than promise.

I began to count backward, hoping sleep would come quickly, but sadness wrapped itself around my chest, slow and suffocating, pressing in until I could barely breathe. I didn't move. I didn't speak. I had learned that silence, like sleep, was a power of resistance. And it drove him crazy.

The silence made him uneasy because, deep down, he knew he was wrong. The weight of my disappointment was written across my face, even if I tried to hide it in my heart.

I wanted him to sit in it, to feel what I felt. My silence wasn't empty. It was filled with everything I didn't say, and in that moment I held onto it with all my might. By the time the roosters crowed again, we were preparing to leave for the harbor.

****

The morning air hung heavy with a stillness that was never truly quiet. By then, word had already spread through the neighborhood. In Cuba, you could not simply leave. You had to declare it. Once our names were on the list, everyone knew. I kept my eyes on the ground as we stepped outside. Across the narrow street, a few neighbors stood in their doorways, whispering.

Others watched from behind half closed shutters, their faces barely visible through the slats. The government called them actos de repudio, acts of repudiation. Neighbors were expected to shout insults at those who chose to leave, to call us traitors, to throw eggs or worse.

That morning a small crowd gathered, but the tension was unmistakable. I felt betrayed and deeply hurt. These were people we knew well. Our children went to school together and played in the same streets. When they had no food, we shared what little we had. We leaned on each other in difficult times. Now everything felt different. Tears blurred my vision as I held the children close. I squeezed Guillermo's hand, holding on tightly, and silently prayed that we would reach the harbor safely.

****

The harbor at Mariel was west of Havana and had become a port of desperation and hope. On April 20, 1980, following protests in Havana and mounting pressure on the Communist regime, Fidel Castro decided to open the port, allowing anyone who wanted to leave to flee the island, including among them the mentally insane and the criminals, "the undesirables," he touted on national television. Over the next few months, more than 125,000 people, my family among them, crossed the Florida Straits in old, overcrowded vessels, praying for a future we could only imagine.

We did not have passports. Ordinary Cubans did not have such things in those days. Passports were reserved for diplomats, athletes traveling for competitions, or students sent abroad by the government. People like us never expected to see one. Instead, the authorities issued what they called a salvoconducto, a safe conduct pass that allowed us to leave the country through Mariel. The paper they gave us was simple, almost temporary, but it was the only thing standing between us and the harbor. I folded the document carefully and held it close, knowing that this small piece of paper carried the weight of our entire future.

We left with nothing more than the clothes on our backs as we boarded the massive vessel bound ninety miles north for the Florida Keys. Standing on the dock with Guillermo and our two children, the reality of the moment felt surreal. All around us, people of every age, entire families, scrambled desperately to claim a space, as if their very lives depended on it.

My son Antonio stood frozen in the whirlwind of farewells, his tiny fingers gripping Guillermo's pant leg like an anchor. He didn't say a word, just held on, as if letting go would sweep him away from everything he knew.

My first-born Karime, who was two years older than her brother, Antonio pressed herself against me, her hand wrapped so tightly around mine I could feel the flutter of her heartbeat. Her almond-shaped eyes locked on the shimmering turquoise waves ahead, but her thoughts were behind us with the cousins, friends, neighbors, and especially her grandfather, Guillo, whom we had just left behind.

I whispered to them both that, in time, they would find new friends. Antonio didn't answer. He just rubbed his face against my stomach, a gesture that said everything his little heart couldn't yet put into words.

I held on to my rosary and a small, knitted pouch, *el paquetico* that *mi padrino* had prepared for me. He'd instructed me to pin it to the inside of my dress, close to my heart, for safe passage. My protector, Yemayá, the Yoruba Goddess of the Ocean, had never steered me wrong.

When I turned to Guillermo, I saw the tears gathered in his eyes. He pulled me into his arms and began sobbing deep, inconsolable cries. I tried to stay strong for our family's sake, but the tears came anyway. I knew exactly what he was experiencing. We didn't need words. We were both dreaming of what awaited us.

America, in our minds, was a magical place with endless possibilities, a land where Guillermo, a mechanical engineer, could find steady work, and perhaps I, an *enfermera*, could earn a few hours' pay, just enough not to miss the moments that mattered most with my children. I knew the transition wouldn't be easy, but anything felt better than living under the weight of fear and uncertainty.

As the boat surged through the busy waters and the shoreline of Cuba began to disappear into the horizon, on the vessel pure mayhem ensued. People were crammed into every inch of space. A man became violently seasick and began vomiting so badly that a fight broke out nearby. Guillermo positioned himself in front of us, shielding us with his body. A woman began praying loudly, her sobs uncontrollable. The fear in her eyes drew everyone's attention, including mine. I wondered if she, too, was afraid of what America might hold. I pressed the *rosario* to my chest, whispered Yemayá's name, and dared to believe that blessings might be waiting on the other side.

****

When we arrived in Miami, a massive crowd had gathered as our boat pulled into the dock. Families embraced, reunited with loved ones they hadn't seen in years, but not everyone was there to welcome us with open arms. Some held banners that screamed "Go Home, We Don't Want You Here," and others hurled insults.

I was stunned by their anger, by the raw, unfiltered hatred etched across their faces. After everything we had endured just to make it there, I never imagined we'd be met with such hostility. For a moment, I questioned whether we had made the right decision.

We moved carefully through the crowds, searching for my aunt, someone I hadn't seen in years. I was so appreciative of her support and her helping my family. She was the one who had coordinated everything from the Miami side. Through relatives and friends, she made sure we knew which vessel to board and where to find it among the hundreds of boats filling the harbor. Without her guidance, we would have been lost in the chaos of Mariel. She also vouched for us to the American government, signing documents that validated our sponsorship and confirmed that we would have support once we arrived.

Truthfully, I could barely remember what she looked like. My children held on to me, wide-eyed and frightened.

"Mami," my daughter whispered, "why are those people angry?"

"I don't know, baby," I replied gently.

"Que se vayan pal carajo," Guillermo uttered under his breath. Antonio, of course, repeated the words, and I shot Guillermo a look, silently urging him to stop before our son turned it into a chant.

I was worried about Guillermo. The commotion when we left had already shaken him. It took everything in me to keep him from responding to the people we thought were our friends. He was never one to start trouble, but he had never been the kind of man to back down from a fight.

As we made our way through the crowd, I held my breath, bracing for anything. We approached a large tent where new arrivals were being registered, and a petite woman with a caramel complexion and tightly curled afro, wearing a flowered cotton dress, stepped into our path.

"Rosa?" she called.

"Tía!" We shouted each other's names aloud, threw our arms around one another, and cried. In that moment, all the noise and chaos faded. Her hug felt like home. She looked so much like my deceased mother that it took my breath away.

Guillermo and the kids lit up when they saw her. We were all tired and hungry and hadn't eaten since morning, so we wasted no time.

"Let's go home and get something to eat," Tia said, her voice warm and steady.

"Say no more," Guillermo replied with a smile, and without missing a beat. The children erupted into cheers.

* * * *

"Vamos a almorzar," mi tía said, as we gathered around her mahogany dining table, draped in a crisp cream-colored cloth and brightened by a vase of fresh hibiscus from her garden. A beautiful

light fixture stood above our heads on the ceiling, illuminating the room.

The taupe-colored wall behind us was graced by an elegant china cabinet that nearly spanned its length, its shelves lined with delicate porcelain plates and cups. "Only for special occasions," *mi tía* boasted.

Sunlight streamed through the lace curtains, casting soft patterns across the plastic-covered couches in the living room adjacent to the dining room. The rich aroma of *congrí*, a traditional dish of white rice and red kidney beans that originated in Oriente, Cuba, where my mom's side of the family was from, permeated the space. Though my children were accustomed to eating *congrí* with white rice and black beans, that didn't stop them from devouring the *congrí* that mingled with the sweetness of *plátano maduro* caramelizing at the edges and the savory *fricase de pollo* simmering to tenderness, each scent tugging at our hunger.

Mi tía set before us heaping plates of food with a colorful salad: crimson colored tomato slices, crisp lettuce, onions, and *aguacate* still cool from the wash, all lightly tossed with salt, vinegar, and oil. She followed with tall glasses of lemonade, chilled and sweet, condensation sliding down the sides.

I couldn't remember the last time I had seen *esa cantidad de comida* gathered on one table. Every bite tasted like home, carrying me back to childhood. I looked over at Guillermo, whose eyes were closed as he savored the flavors, and then at my children, whose eyes widened at the sight of the homemade flan, the custard topped with a glossy veil of caramel, its golden syrup cascading down the sides and pooling onto the plate.

I chuckled at the innocent wonder on their faces, and that afternoon, I ate two full plates. Guillermo did the same, and even my picky little eaters finished every bite without protest. Later, with our bellies full, we dozed off on the couch in front of the television in her living room until the rich aroma of freshly brewed *café* roused us awake.

****

Mi tía, a widow, lived in a modest single-story home in Carol City, a neighborhood made up mostly of African-American families: postal workers, teachers, and civil servants who took pride in their lawns and greeted each other by name. Three palm trees stood tall in her front yard, their fronds swaying gently in the breeze, while avocado and mango trees flourished out back, their branches weighed heavy with fruit, and bright hibiscus blooms framed the house in bursts of red and coral.

"The neighborhood has changed a lot," *tia* explained. "My neighbors two doors down moved north to Broward County. There have been a few break-ins in the area," she said with a concerned look, and then she smiled. "But this is home, and it'll be my home until the good Lord calls me."

My cousin Yasmine begged *mi tia*, her mom, to move in with her family or consider moving to a safer neighborhood. But my aunt wouldn't hear of it. She felt rooted there. Everyone knew her, and even the neighborhood children waved as they passed by. *Mi tia* was a retiree from Miami-Dade County Public Schools after thirty years of service as a math teacher.

So much of Miami reminded me of Cuba: the food, the culture, the people, yet it was undeniably a world apart. Here, people spoke freely and openly about their disappointment in the government, something we could never dare do back home. And the access to everything, both the good and the bad, was overwhelming.

The men and women seemed so polished, so effortlessly elegant. The women were striking, and for a moment, I felt self-conscious. I was thinner than most of the women I saw strolling about in the city, their curves commanding attention. *Mi tía* reassured me that the weight would come with time, but in the same breath, she warned me not to let it get away from me. "*Recuerda, mija*," she said more than once, "*el azúcar y la presión*, are in our blood." She reminded me so much of my mother. She spoke the kind of wisdom that was passed down in kitchens, between sips of café and deep conversations.

Her daughter Yasmine and her son-in-law, Pedro, were both respected surgeons at the University of Miami Hospital, where they also taught residency courses. Their home in Coral Gables was unlike anything I had ever seen: elegant and sprawling, with manicured lawns and tree-lined streets that screamed wealth. The contrast between their neighborhood and *mi tía's* modest barrio in Carol City was stark, almost jarring. The neighborhoods were segregated, with affluent white families living in better areas than people of color.

I was deeply grateful for the clothes and shoes Yasmine had gifted me from her closet, graceful, stylish pieces she no longer wore but that felt brand new to me. Pedro had also gathered a few things for Guillermo: a couple of polo shirts, denim jeans, sneakers, slacks, shorts, and even a suit and a pair of shoes. They bought clothes for the children, too, along with a few toys to keep their hands and minds occupied. Yasmine even offered to take Karime and Antonio to her house for the weekend, giving Guillermo and me a chance to rest and get settled.

It wasn't just the clothes or the toys that I appreciated; it was the kind gesture. The acknowledgment that we were starting over, and that they were willing to help us do so with a measure of dignity.

Yasmine was the spitting image of *mi tio* José: sharp-featured, with a pointed nose and thin lips that whispered of old Spanish bloodlines.

Mi tia told us a story of when Yasmine was born. Tia said she just stared at Yasmine in disbelief, half-convinced the hospital had handed her the wrong baby. There wasn't a hint of color on her, not even the soft curve of her earlobe bore our family's bronze undertones. With porcelain skin and eyes like cut emeralds, Yasmine moved through the world cloaked in a privilege she never had to ask for. She passed for white without effort, often without even knowing she'd done it.

Her husband, Pedro, came to the United States in 1960 as a young exile. He attended Christopher Columbus High, the kind of prep school where boys are trained to dominate competitively in boardrooms and rarely hear the word "no." At the University of Florida, he crossed paths with Yasmine, and together they looked like something out of a high-society wedding spread: Pedro, with his golden hair, chiseled jaw, and pale alabaster skin, completed the picture of privilege.

Pedro was polite but distant. He would speak to me in Spanish, then switch to English when addressing Guillermo, which felt strange. It was a small thing, but I noticed it. Yasmine had to remind him more than once that Guillermo spoke fluent Spanish. There was a chill beneath Pedro's politeness, too, a stiffness in how he greeted us. He was never rude, never obvious, but I knew how to read a man who'd drawn a line. And I had a strong feeling he'd already placed Guillermo on the other side of one.

Mi tía took us everywhere with her: errands, visits, and even the supermarket, Winn-Dixie. It was the first time Guillermo and I had ever seen so much food in one place. Aisles stretched endlessly, overflowing with meats, produce, choices, and abundance. We stood in disbelief, overwhelmed by what others seemed to take for granted.

Even the kids noticed the difference. Karime stared at the shelves, her brow furrowed in confusion. "Mami, how much are we allowed to take? Where's the line? And how come you don't have *la libreta*?" she asked, still trying to understand a place where food was not counted or rationed.

I chuckled. "No, *mi hija*. They don't use *la libreta* here."

Karime looked around, her eyes wide and curious. I leaned down and spoke softly. "You see all these people, *corazón*? They're here to buy food for their families, too. Just like us." She smiled, then her face turned serious. "Will there be more when we come back?"

Yeah, there will be plenty more. Hearing my daughter question whether there would be more food in the store made me sad. No child should have to wonder about that. I felt a sense of relief that living in America would begin to reshape her understanding of abundance, of security, of what was possible. All I could do at that moment was thank *Dios*.

Back in Cuba, we were used to long lines, "*La cola*," and ration books, "*la libreta*," our monthly supply of food carefully calculated by the number of mouths in our home. More often than not, it wasn't enough to last the month. We learned to stretch what little we had and make do with discipline.

Karime nodded slowly, accepting my answer in that thoughtful way children do, trusting, even in uncertainty. We turned back to the shelves, hand in hand, and then met up with Guillermo and the others.

****

Guillermo and I lay side by side in Yasmine's childhood bedroom after a long day of sightseeing. Yasmine's bedroom walls were covered in posters, a shrine to pop culture faces we didn't recognize, except for one: Michael Jackson. The pale pink walls with posters felt like a maze of '70s rock idols.

Guillermo got up and turned off the television. It had long since stopped entertaining us and was now just flickering in the background, watching us instead. He slipped back into bed and pulled me toward him, his head resting gently between my thighs as he began kissing me passionately, softly and slowly. His lips moved with care. He took my nipple into his mouth, tugging gently, tenderly, as if reminding me that I was still wanted, still his.

"Te amo, Rosita, no te olvides."

"Oijiste? Si, Guillermo, I said softly. I climbed on top of him and stroked his face with my hand. My hair fell and cascaded down my back. His hands gripped my hips instinctively, and his moaning grew deeper, more urgent, as we found a rhythm that was both familiar and needed.

After all these years, Guillermo's sweet cacao skin color, his beautiful smile, and towering six feet three inch frame never failed to do it for me. He always made me feel desired, even after having his children.

The stretch marks that lay bare on my hips didn't deter him, either. If anything, he was drawn to them like they were something to be celebrated. We ended the night asleep in each other's arms.

Chapter 2

"Bemba Colora"

Guillermo and I woke up to the smell of bacon, eggs, toast, *plátano maduro*, and freshly squeezed orange juice. The kids were already up, bathed, dressed for the day, and buzzing with excitement to try pancakes for the first time. They loved every bite and begged my aunt to make them again every morning.

She would drizzle a teaspoon of thick, sweetened condensed milk with a splash of syrup, the sugary blend clinging to the spoon. For Antonio, she blended the creamy richness of *batido de mamey*, and for Karime, the bright freshness of *fruta bomba*. With each small gesture, the kitchen filled with comfort, making them feel truly at home.

"Did you guys say thank you to *mi tía*?" I asked.

Their faces lit up. "Yes!" they shouted in unison, their excitement spilling over.

Seeing how well my children were adjusting to life in America brought me a deep sense of relief. Guillermo loved it here, too, though I could tell a piece of his heart still longed for Cuba. Even so, we both knew that leaving had been the right decision.

While my aunt was genuinely happy to have us, Guillermo and I knew it was time to start looking for work and a place of our own. The kids would need to be enrolled in school soon.

"You can stay as long as you want," Tia announced over breakfast. "I have more than enough room for all of you. You're not a bother to me." I knew *mi tia* enjoyed our company, especially with the kids. They rarely came to us for anything while she was present in the home.

I knew the kids definitely weren't ready to leave, especially after Guillermo cleaned and repaired *mi tia's* pool. As a thank you, he took care of anything he could around the house: leaky faucets, broken tiles, even the sagging back fence. It was his way of showing appreciation for everything she had done for us.

****

Later that evening, we met up with Isabelle and Alberto, a couple we had known since high school, now living in New Jersey. Word of our arrival in Miami had somehow reached one of their relatives, who called my aunt to arrange a visit. I hadn't expected to see them, and yet there they were, stepping into the restaurant patio like a pair of ghosts from our previous life.

Isabelle had changed. Not in spirit, she still carried that warm smile and playful glint in her eyes, but physically, she was nearly unrecognizable. She'd gained a lot of weight. Her once-slim frame was softer now, fuller. Still beautiful, just…bigger.

Alberto had changed, too. His belly rounded slightly over his belt, and his face had grown noticeably fuller. They both looked older than thirty-two, more tired, maybe. Or maybe that was just life in America.

"Asere, qué bolá!" we shouted, hugging and laughing, our eyes wide with disbelief at how quickly time had passed. They pulled out their wallets and proudly showed us photos of their home, a lovely place nestled in a New Jersey neighborhood, just right for their two kids, who happened to be the same ages as ours. Seeing their children smiling, settled, and happy stirred something in me.

Not in an envious way, but I wanted that for us too. For the first time, I felt encouraged. Maybe we could have that kind of life. I looked over at Guillermo and smiled, and he gave me a knowing smile in return—the kind that said he was thinking the same thing.

We had dinner outdoors, under a canopy of palm trees that swayed in the warm breeze. The air smelled faintly of salt and citrus, the kind of scent that only a coastal city like Miami could offer. Laughter came easily, and so did the food and drinks. And when the bill came, no one let us pay a dime.

Mi tía had given Guillermo some money that morning, enough to cover both lunch and dinner, just in case. But it turned out to be unnecessary. The kindness of those around us was overwhelming. We were surrounded by generosity, and it was humbling.

We spent the first hour swapping stories and catching up on gossip from home. Whose cousin had gotten married, who had gotten divorced, and who had moved to the States. It felt like peeling back the curtain on a world we'd only recently left behind.

Eventually, the conversation moved, as it always did, to our plans.

"So, what's next for you two?" Isabelle asked gently, taking a sip of her mojito.

Guillermo and I exchanged a look. We didn't have an answer. Not one that felt real, or ready. We'd only been in Miami for two weeks, still navigating this unfamiliar life one day at a time. But people always wanted to know. I wasn't sure if it was an American thing that they craved a destination, a timeline, a plan that made sense on paper. And we were expected to have answers, even when we were still figuring out the questions. It was the same with the social workers we had met earlier that week, polite smiles paired with eyes that seemed to measure every word and movement.

I offered a gentle smile and changed the conversation. "So, how come you two aren't living in Miami?" I asked, turning toward Isabelle. For me, Miami felt like being in Cuba, so it felt strange that any Cuban would consider living anywhere else but Miami. I was stunned by their responses.

Isabelle glanced at Alberto and smirked. "I love everything about Miami," she said, her tone light. "The weather, the food, the people… But the money? The money's up north."

Alberto nodded, the tension in his jaw betraying something deeper. His voice grew louder. "Cost of living is too high here and the pay doesn't match," he said. "What I make as a contractor in Paterson is nearly three to four times what I'd get paid down here."

I nodded, the weight of his words settling into my chest. So many of life's choices were dictated by money. You could dream in color, but reality still handed you the blueprint in black and white. I guess that's capitalism.

Still, for a moment, beneath the gentle rustle of palm fronds and the clink of ice swirling in our glasses, it felt like anything was possible.

"You should come work for me," Alberto said out of nowhere, turning to Guillermo. "I could use the help, and I know I can count on you. There's a nursing school nearby, too. Rosa could enroll."

After receiving a nod from Isabelle, he added, "There are good schools in the area."

"Do they offer English classes?" I asked.

"Yeah. Year-round."

"You'll never learn English if you stay here, except for the kids, as they'll be in school," Isabelle said gently, her voice firm but kind.

I watched cartoons with the kids in English so I could start learning too. I was amazed at how much they had picked up in such a short time, and their eagerness to learn had surprised me.

I looked over at Guillermo. He smiled, but didn't respond right away, his eyes fixed on something in the distance, focused, yet far away. I could tell by his expression that he was just as overwhelmed as I was. We both knew our lives were changing right before our eyes.

"You'll get used to the cold," Isabelle continued. "It's not that bad. And you'll get to experience all four seasons."

When Alberto mentioned how much he'd pay Guillermo each week, my husband's eyes lit up like a kid in a candy shop, and I could see that he was ready to accept the offer on the spot. I was stunned too, but I gently tapped his leg under the table so that he wouldn't give Alberto an answer right away. We needed time to discuss this move.

When Alberto and Isabelle drove us back to my tia's house, we promised we would be in touch soon with a decision. As we walked toward the door, hand in hand, the question still remained in the back of my mind. It was like a train in the distance that you can hear coming, but you're not sure if you're ready to board.

****

Yasmine picked up the kids and took them to her place for the weekend, giving Guillermo and me a rare moment of time alone. The house, usually alive with laughter, footsteps, and constant motion, settled into a gentle stillness. There was no rush, no pressure, just space to breathe, to think, to speak honestly about what might come next. It was the first time since arriving that we had a real chance to reflect without distraction.

After making some café, *mi tia* and I made our way to the Florida room, a space she'd added to the back of the house nearly twenty years ago. Her sanctuary. Her "jungle peace," she affectionately called it. The room overflowed with life: ferns spilling from ceramic pots, orchids perched on wicker stands, pothos vines trailing across the windows. A large statue of Santa Barbara, the patron saint of Cuba, stood nestled among the plants, holding a sword in her hand and a red cloak draped over her shoulders.

Sunlight filtered through bamboo shades, casting golden streaks across the tiled floor. The air smelled of damp soil, jasmine, and mint, while a nearby radio played light music.

Mi tía and I stood by the window, watching as sweat poured down Guillermo's face. He was kneeling beside one of the larger pots, carefully replanting a hibiscus that had outgrown its container. His hands, always steady and deliberate, worked the soil with a kind of reverence as if tending to the roots might somehow help him plant himself more firmly in this unfamiliar life.

Mi tia eased into her wicker rocking chair, its cushions faded from years of sun. Her bare feet slipped into her *chancletas* with the ease of ritual. "You have a good man," Tia said as she peered out the window. "Sit, *mija*," she said, patting the seat beside her. "Tell me what's really on your mind."

I sat down, and for the first time all day, I exhaled. "It hasn't always been easy being his wife," I said.

"*Mija*, no marriage is perfect."

While I gathered my thoughts, she studied me. "How was dinner with Albertico and Isabelle?"

"It was great," I said, nodding. "We ate at a beautiful restaurant and the meal was delicious. It felt good, familiar. For a moment, it was like we never left Cuba."

Mi tía rocked slowly, her eyes fixed on the garden outside. "Familiar doesn't always mean safe, *mija*. Or right."

I gathered my thoughts. The silence between us wasn't heavy—it was generous, open, like she was giving me space to go deeper.

"They invited us to come to New Jersey to live," I said finally. "Alberto offered Guillermo a job. Said I could enroll in a nursing program nearby."

"And?" *mi tia* asked, her voice gentle but steady.

I hesitated. "Guillermo seems interested. The money's better, the schools are good… It's a real opportunity. But I'm not sure."

"Is it the cold?" she asked with a knowing smile.

I shook my head. "No. It's…everything else. Starting over again. Leaving the kids with new faces, new places, another version of the unfamiliar. I'm just starting to feel my feet touch the ground here. I'm scared to uproot that."

She nodded, then reached for her *cafecito* and took a small sip. "Fear is normal. But don't confuse fear with discernment. *Dios* sometimes speaks through restlessness, through uncertainty. But sometimes He speaks through peace. Through stillness."

Her words sank into me like water into dry earth. "You won't fail your family by choosing what gives you peace," she continued. "You've already done the hardest thing by leaving Cuba and everything behind. Now it's about listening for what's next."

I looked out the window at Guillermo, who had moved on to trimming the edges of the garden, his brow still furrowed in focus. I could see the weight he carried. Maybe he, too, was trying to listen.

"I just don't want to make a decision I'll regret."

"You won't," she said, reaching over to squeeze my hand.

Guillermo came inside, drenched in sweat, tracking a trail of dirt onto the rug on the porch. He wiped his brow, then eased down beside me, the scent of soil and sunlight still clinging to his skin.

"*Mi tía* thinks we should consider the move to New Jersey. It could be good for us," I said gently.

"Whatever decision you make, I will support you either way," *mi tia* quickly interjected with a huge smile.

A slow smile spread across his face. "I think it would be a great opportunity for us too," he replied, reaching for her hand. "But I'm going to miss you, *mi tia*." His voice cracked, and for a moment, he couldn't speak. Tears slipped silently down his cheeks.

Mi tía squeezed his hand, her eyes misty. "You'll do just fine. Both of you. Just don't forget where you came from and who's always praying for you."

Guillermo nodded, clearing his throat. "When we get settled, we want you to come visit us," he said, his voice soft but certain.

She smiled, full of grace and pride. "I will, *mijo.*

Chapter 3

"Ríe y Llora"

It was a somber day. Everything was packed, and we were ready to embark on the long drive to Patterson, New Jersey. *Mi tía* had prepared enough food to feed an army, carefully wrapped in aluminum foil, each bundle a gesture of love and care for the road ahead.

We had arrived with next to nothing, and now, somehow, we were leaving with suitcases full of clothes, toiletries, toys, and things that we needed. I hoped it would all fit into Alberto's car.

Just as we were preparing to load the last bag, Yasmine pulled into the driveway. She stepped out of the car and handed me an envelope.

"Prima," she said gently, "this is just a small token of my appreciation for you and Guillermo for taking such good care of my mom. This should hold you over for a while. Pedro sends his love."

I opened it and saw the stack of bills, folded neatly and secured with a rubber band. My hands trembled. The tears came streaming fast and unexpectedly. I couldn't speak, could only nod through the wave of emotion that rose in my chest. It wasn't just the money—it was what it represented: kindness, gratitude, and a reminder that we were not alone.

I could barely get the words out. I was so choked up with emotion, I could hardly contain myself.

"Thank you, *prima*, for everything you've done for my family. *Somos familia*," she added. "*Gracias a ti por todo*."

Guillermo stepped forward and hugged Yasmine. He, too, was overcome with emotion. "*Gracias, prima*," he whispered, his voice cracking. He then signaled the kids to say their goodbyes, and they, too, were in tears. As we drove away, they kept looking back, their eyes fixed on *mi tía*, who stood at the edge of the driveway, waving until we disappeared from view.

As we headed toward the interstate, the news came through the radio that an all-white, all-male jury had acquitted four White Miami-Dade police officers in the savage, senseless beating death of Arthur McDuffie, an unarmed Black insurance salesman, a father and former Marine.

McDuffie was chased down by police on December 17, 1979, while riding his motorcycle. What followed was a brutal beating that left the thirty-three-year-old former Marine clinging to life. He lay in a coma for days before finally dying from his wounds. The case drew much media attention and stirred such raw racial tension that the judge moved the trial to Tampa in the hope of finding something closer to justice.

When the verdict was announced on the radio, it hit like a punch to the chest. *Mi tia* had been following the case closely, and she was praying for justice for McDuffie. Soon after discussing it with her, we began tracking the story ourselves *en el noticiario*.

I looked over at Guillermo to see that his jaw was tight, his eyes locked straight ahead. A heavy silence settled over the car, thick and suffocating, as if even the air had turned against us. We didn't know all the details of the case, but the frustration etched into the faces of the crowd was something we understood all too well.

"¿Cuál es la diferencia entre McDuffie y yo? Soy negro y un papá," Guillermo said angrily.

"Ninguna," Alberto replied, his voice heavy with sorrow.

By the time we turned onto NW 62nd Street, we were no longer in the city we had come to know. We were in the center of an uprising. Miami was burning. Plumes of smoke stretched above rooftops. Angry crowds flooded the streets, barricading intersections, hurling bottles, and flipping trash cans. Storefronts exploded into shards of glass. The rhythm of chaos beat all around us.

My children's voices cut through the tension, and they began to ask so many questions. "Mami, what's happening?"

"Why are people yelling?"

"Are we in trouble?"

I couldn't answer. I didn't know how.

A mob surged near the station wagon, fists raised, faces twisted in fury and anguish. Shouts and sirens echoed around us. This wasn't just a protest—it was a heartbreak in motion, a city wailing from a wound that never healed.

"We can't move anywhere," Alberto uttered, his voice tight with tension. The car was boxed in, surrounded on all sides.

Isabelle gripped the back of her seat, her eyes wide with fear. I could feel the panic rising in my chest, sharp, breathless, unrelenting. Guillermo saw it, too.

"I hope *mi tia* is safe."

"I'll call her," he said, trying to keep us all calm.

"How?" I asked, my voice barely above a whisper.

"I'll find a payphone."

"It's not safe," I said, grabbing his arm, afraid that if he stepped outside, he might not come back.

So, we sat trapped in the thick of history and horror for two long, terrifying hours. The children huddled close. Isabelle wept quietly. Alberto's hands trembled on the steering wheel. We were stranded between where we'd come from and where we were trying to go, praying the storm would pass before it swallowed us whole.

As night fell, we managed to cut through the chaos and make our way back to *mi tia* house. We knocked several times before the door creaked open. She peered through the window first, her face etched with worry. It turned out that she'd been glued to the news, her eyes swollen from tears and sleeplessness.

"Gracias a Dios," she whispered, ushering us inside. My tía had been praying. A white candle glowed on her altar, surrounded by *los santos*, fresh flowers, and glasses of water placed there for the spirits.

Yasmine and Pedro were safe, she assured us. They had stayed at the hospital, where things were tense but secure.

May 17, 1980, became a date that would forever be etched in my memory. The riots went on for four days. By the end, eighteen lives were lost, and millions of dollars in property lay in ruins. The city was scorched, but it wasn't just buildings that burned. It was trust, hope, and the fragile illusion that justice could prevail.

We were so afraid another uprising might erupt that we avoided the city streets altogether and jumped on the nearest highway, heading north as soon as we could.

****

I was elated when I saw the sign that read "Welcome to New Jersey," even though we were all still reeling over the riots. It was like a never-ending nightmare that looped in my mind.

Everything about New Jersey felt different, even the vegetation. The trees looked older, the leaves dull and muted, stripped of the vibrant colors we were used to. Everyone we passed seemed to be rushing, either to their cars or to catch a bus, desperate to escape the rainy dreary day in May. The pace felt faster than Miami's, but cold in more ways than one. As we got closer to the city, I noticed trash scattered along the streets. It was as if no one cared, or felt any urgency, to throw garbage into an actual bin.

Eventually, we arrived at Alberto and Isabelle's beautiful home, nestled in the suburbs. Exhausted but hopeful, we stepped out of the car and stretched our stiff arms and legs after nearly twenty-four hours on the road.

The savory aroma of garlic, cilantro, and carne asada drifted through the air. Their children came running out, squealing with excitement. Isabelle's mother welcomed us with open arms, while her grandchildren eagerly led my kids upstairs to play, like little seasoned hosts.

The living room felt cozy and familiar with oversized furniture wrapped in protective plastic, a television nestled inside a polished wooden cabinet, and a fire crackling in the fireplace. Isabelle gave me a quick tour of the house: four bedrooms, two bathrooms, all set on two acres of land. The kids shared a room with bunk beds, while Isabelle and Alberto had their own room, and her parents slept in another. The final room doubled as a guest space and home office.

After dinner, they took us to their nearby rental property, our new home, for now. It was a modest duplex with two bedrooms and one bathroom, fully furnished, which brought a wave of relief. We wouldn't need to do much to settle in. There was even a washer and dryer, something I wasn't used to having back in Cuba. After a few days of handwashing, I gave the washer a try and never looked back. From that point on, it was *la lavadora* all the way.

The kids were thrilled to finally have their own space, racing to claim their beds with laughter and excitement. I set to work right away, changing linens, wiping down walls and counters, scrubbing the bathroom, refrigerator, and stove, and mopping the floors until the whole apartment felt clean and new.

With an incense I'd bought from a Botanica in Miami, I walked slowly from room to room, letting the smoke curl through the air to drive out any bad spirits and invite blessings in. In the corner of the pantry, I created a small altar in honor of Oshun, inviting sweetness, love, and blessings to take root in our new home.

Guillermo teased me that I was turning into an American woman overnight. Maybe I was, but some things had simply become more practical for the life we were trying to build. Besides, this was the first time in our marriage that I didn't have to depend on my husband. I had my own dreams and aspirations.

With the money Yasmine gifted us, we were able to purchase a used car. Nothing fancy, but something that could get us to our destinations with ease. Guillermo came home around 6:00 p.m. every evening, and our children had started attending the same school as Alberto's kids, which made the transition a little easier for all of us. I took an English class that met twice a week, and I was actively looking for a job.

Each morning, I woke up early to prepare breakfast and iron Guillermo and the kids' clothes. I would also prepare their lunches to carry to work and school. Guillermo would drop them off at school on his way to the office, while I stayed behind to clean and start dinner. By noon, I was heading out to class, catching the city bus with a notebook in hand, my purse, and a prayer in my heart. After class, I'd ride the bus home, often tired. Life was busy, unfamiliar, and far from easy, but it was ours, and we were making it work one day at a time.

Riding the city bus in America was a different experience altogether. The Black American women were stunning, bold in their style and full of expression, whether through their clothes, their jewelry, or the things they said or didn't say. I admired their confidence and wished I had even a fraction of it.

Every day, I saw the same faces on the bus. Over time, we began to greet one another with nods, smiles, and the occasional kind word. A few times, when I was running late and sprinted to catch the bus, other passengers would shout for the driver to wait. As I climbed aboard, breathless, I'd hear a woman call out, "Hey girl!" and I'd smile, feeling a little less like a stranger. Little by little, I started picking up words, piecing together meanings, and slowly building a sense of belonging.

Chapter 4

"Azúcar Negra"

That first winter in Patterson was unforgiving. One day, as I stepped onto the city bus, a petite woman with gorgeous hair handed me a business card.

"¿De dónde eres?"

"Soy Cubana."

"¡Ay, qué bueno! Ven a mi salón."

Carmen was Dominican, and just like that, we became friends. She would stop by the house whenever she had time. We both had children, though she wasn't with her children's father. On Saturdays, she'd sometimes wash and blow-dry my hair. Most of the time, she didn't charge me, and she paid me to help clean her salon.

Carmen's salon sat between a bodega and a laundromat, its glass door outlined with hand-painted lettering, the corners now curling with age. Inside the shop, the air was warm and fragrant, thick with the sizzle of flat irons, the rich scent of hair straighteners, keratin treatments, and coconut oil, and the bold aroma of Dominican coffee brewing in the back. Women with oversized rollers sat beneath hooded dryers, magazines spread open across their laps, their faces half-hidden behind glossy magazine pages and rising steam.

The sound of hair dryers blended with bachata music playing loud from a stereo, while women moved their hands expressively as they spoke, their voices dancing with laughter and bursts of English in between.

Carmen reminded me of the women in Havana who never apologized for taking up space.

"Sit, *mija*," Carmen said, patting the red vinyl chair with a quick smile. "I'm gonna wash that Cuban stress out of your scalp."

I laughed nervously and slid into the chair. Around me, women moved like they belonged, tossing hair towels as they flipped through tattered magazines. There was an ease in how they carried themselves, how they spoke, how they claimed space without apology. I watched them, wondering if I could ever move like that and be that free.

As Carmen massaged shampoo into my scalp, I closed my eyes and exhaled for what felt like the first time all week.

"You remind me of me when I first got here," she said. "Didn't know nobody. English sounded like *uno disco* scratched up. Now look. I run this place, and people wait in line for me."

She chuckled as she rinsed my hair. "Takes time, but you'll see. This country don't give you nothing. But it will teach you how to take."

Carmen quickly became my confidant. I valued her advice and admired her strength. Guillermo, however, wasn't thrilled about the changes he saw in me or about my growing friendship with Carmen. To him, she was a threat. She didn't have a man at home helping her, and yet, she managed everything on her own. It wasn't that she didn't want a partner—she just hadn't found the right one. Until then, she carried the weight of it all herself.

It didn't help that I'd gained about thirty pounds, all in the right places, according to Guillermo. He said I looked beautiful, but I could sense his unease. My independence was blossoming, and it made him unsure of where he stood. I had started wearing a little makeup, not much, just enough to feel a difference when I looked in the mirror.

Sometimes, men would flirt with me. I'd smile politely, and in my heavily broken English, I'd reply, "Thank you, I happy married." And I meant it. But for the first time in a long time, I also meant something else. I was a woman who was beginning to see her own worth.

****

The weather was finally breaking, *gracias a Dios*. Spring arrived slowly that year, as if even the season needed time to adjust to New Jersey.

We no longer needed coats, and the vegetation slowly began returning to its original colors. People gathered on stoops, blasting music and soaking in their idea of warmth.

Winters in Paterson stretched on so long that there were mornings I stood at the bus stop unable to feel my face, my toes numb inside my boots. My skin grew pale and dry, so I kept a small bottle of lotion and Vaseline tucked in my purse. We were constantly coming down with colds, first the kids, then me and Guillermo. On the coldest mornings, I slipped into the bodega for warmth, sipping a small café as I waited for the bus. Every so often, I stepped outside to check the street, afraid I might miss it if I stayed too long. When the headlights finally appeared, I ran as fast as I could toward the stop.

The children were bundled in so many layers they could hardly move. Unaccustomed to the chill, they whimpered against the bite of the wind, their noses raw and red, their small hands stiff inside their mittens. At home, I tried to make our space a refuge from the cold that settled deep into our bones. I put on big pots of sopa de pollo, letting the aroma fill the kitchen with comfort. Adjusting to this weather was not easy. Guillermo often said that only the brave could endure the brittle cold. But warmth carried its own price. When the electric bill arrived, it reminded us that comfort always came at a cost in America.

****

Our immediate neighbors were *muy raros*. There was a constant stream of people coming and going from their apartment at all hours. An unusual smell seeped through the vents, and the people who emerged from that unit looked dazed, like they were walking in a trance.

It didn't take long to find out they were using and selling a drug called crack, which had become a devastating force in the community, its grip so strong, it drove people to do unimaginable things. Guillermo installed another lock. I tucked the kids in tighter, but fear still crept in at night.

One afternoon, I came home and saw a woman in the alleyway performing oral sex on a man who barely acknowledged her. I stood frozen in disbelief.

What if my daughter had seen this? Or my son? Would they think this was normal?

My heart sank. I was furious. That was the moment I knew we needed something better. Something safer.

That night, I couldn't sleep. Every creak in the hallway, every car passing outside, every raised voice made my heart race. I lay awake listening to the soft breaths of my children, tucked safely in their beds, and I knew I couldn't keep pretending everything was fine.

We had come too far, survived too much, to let this be our normal.

The next morning, over breakfast, I looked at Guillermo.

"We have to move," I said plainly.

He looked up from his coffee, studying my face. "*Lo sé*," he said quietly. "I've been thinking the same thing."

We didn't have much saved, but that didn't matter. I would clean more salons if I had to. Guillermo could pick up side jobs. We'd figure it out like we always did.

I asked around at church, on the bus, scanned bulletin boards at the grocery store, and talked to Carmen, who seemed to know everyone in the neighborhood.

"Be patient," she told me one afternoon as she swept up the salon floor. "The right place will come. And when it does, you'll find it. I know you want better. You deserve better. And it's coming, *mija*. Just don't settle."

Her words stayed with me. That night, I wrote them down in the back of my English notebook, folded the page, and tucked it into my wallet like a promise.

Guillermo told me he confronted Alberto. "They're a problem," he said. "People in and out at all hours. The smell, the noise. It's not safe for our children."

Alberto sighed. "I hear you, *hermano*. I'll talk to them. But…they pay their rent on time. Every month."

Guillermo told me his face tightened. He pulled out a stack of receipts and slammed them on the table. "So do we. Does our money mean nothing to you?" Then he walked out.

"Guillermo, come back," Alberto called after him. "Let me explain."

True to his word, Alberto spoke to the neighbors. For about two weeks, things quieted down. The traffic slowed, the smells faded, and the nights were peaceful. Then it all started again, louder, darker, and more disruptive than before.

Guillermo grew more frustrated by the day. Whenever the alleyway filled with that same burning smell or someone pounded on the neighbor's door at midnight, Guillermo would sit on the edge of the bed, jaw clenched, staring into the dark.

"I don't feel safe here," he said one night. "Not for you. Not for the kids."

I didn't disagree. I'd begun double-checking the locks, pulling the curtains tight, and sleeping with one ear open. The sound of glass breaking in the alleyway no longer startled me. It only reminded me that we didn't belong here.

Guillermo didn't speak to Alberto for days. They were like family, more like brothers, really, but Guillermo couldn't shake the feeling of betrayal.

"He cares more about rent than respect," Guillermo said as we washed dishes together. "And I don't want to keep explaining to my children why someone passed out in the yard."

"Maybe he's in a tough spot too," I offered. "Maybe he's just…overwhelmed."

"We can't wait around for things to change here. It's time we find a place of our own. Alberto may have personal issues that he's dealing with, but you and our children are my priority."

That weekend, Guillermo picked up an extra shift helping a friend with a construction job. I spent hours cleaning Carmen's salon from top to bottom, scrubbing every corner until my back ached.

We started setting money aside quietly and steadily, doing whatever we could to make our next move possible. Then Yasmine gave me the rest of what we needed, without hesitation and without even asking. I accepted it with gratitude, but also with a knot in my stomach.

I knew Guillermo would be upset. He never wanted Yasmine or *mi tía* to think he wasn't doing enough and that he couldn't provide for his family. For him, it wasn't just about money. It was about pride, about dignity. About being seen as the man of the house. Still, I took it. Not out of disrespect, but out of necessity. Because sometimes, survival doesn't wait for pride to catch up.

****

I sat on the bathroom floor, close enough to reach the toilet each time the urge to vomit hit, which felt like every few seconds.

The kids were at school. Guillermo was at work.

I called Carmen, and she came right away, taking me to a clinic that accepted my state insurance. It was something I was still adjusting to. Back in Cuba, healthcare and education had always been free. Needless to say, I was stunned when the doctor said I was pregnant. A part of me was happy. This would be Guillermo's and my first child born in America. This child would never experience what my other kids had gone through.

But still, I wished it wasn't so soon. I had one more class before applying to the nursing program. I didn't want my pregnancy to interfere with my goals. Then I reminded myself that God knows best.

****

Guillermo came home exhausted. He didn't say much, just leaned in to kiss me, and the scent of rum on his breath sent me running to the bathroom.

"Babe, are you okay?" he called after me.

"I'm fine. I'll be out in a second."

When I finally stepped out, he looked me up and down, studying me.

"You sure you're okay?" he asked, raising a brow.

I nodded, avoiding his stare. "Just a little queasy. Must've been something I ate."

He didn't push, just pulled off his boots and sank into the couch, rubbing his temples. I picked up the boots and stood quietly, wondering if now was the right time to tell him. But something about the heaviness in his shoulders made me hesitate. So, I kept the news to myself.

"You want to take a bath before I heat up dinner?" I asked.

"Sure," he said, his voice low.

I ran his bath, poured in Epsom salt, and watched the steam rise. When he stepped in and closed the door behind him, he pulled me close, his hands sliding down my hips, gently rubbing my breasts.

His caress was exactly what I needed.

"Baby," he whispered, leaning me over the sink.

We made love quietly in the warm, tiled space, not even the sound of little footsteps running down the hallway stopping us.

"Mami!" one of the kids called out. "Where are you?"

"I'm coming," I called back, breathless, a soft smile tugging at my lips.

****

Later that evening, after bathing the kids, tucking them in, and taking a quick shower, Guillermo and I was on the couch watching *Leonela*, the popular Venezuelan telenovela on Telemundo. We were completely hooked. On nights it aired, we ate and raced through the bedtime routine, making sure the kids were sound asleep so nothing would interrupt us. I'd pop a bag of popcorn and pull two cold *maltas* from the fridge. This was our little ritual for the drama we couldn't get enough of.

Even *mi tía* and the women at the salon talked about Pedro Luis and Leonela like they were real people. We counted down the hours until the next episode.

Cable had just started gaining popularity in major cities across the U.S., and with over fifty channels from all over the world, it felt like a luxury. We paid a little extra each month for it, but to us, it was worth every penny.

That night's episode was so good, I figured it was the perfect time to tell Guillermo we were expecting.

"Honey, I have a surprise for you," I said, nudging him.

"What kind of surprise?"

"No, guess."

"Baby, just tell me."

"We're having a baby."

He sat up straight, a serious look on his face. For a moment, he just stared at me. Then, slowly, a smile spread across his lips.

"I know we can't really afford it," I added quickly. "I'm almost done with my class and—"

"Listen," he said, taking my hand. "A baby is a blessing. We'll make do." He paused. "I found a new place. It's not too far from Alberto. It's a single-family house in a good neighborhood. We don't have to change schools. The owner said he might sell it to us in a few years. I already placed a deposit, and we can move in at the start of the month."

"That's amazing," I said. "Let's call *mi tia* and tell her the good news!" Then I hesitated. "Well… Before we do, there's something I should tell you. Yasmine gave us some money toward the new place."

He stiffened. "Why did you ask her?"

"I didn't. She offered," I said softly.

Guillermo looked disappointed, his eyes dropping for a moment.

"Baby, please don't be upset," I whispered. "They're proud of us. They just want to help."

"*Mi vida*, I'm a man, my family is my responsibility," he said, his voice steady but thick with emotion. "Don't minimize my role. I'm not just here to take up space. I'm not your roommate, I'm your husband. I'm the father of your children."

He paused, then softened. "I love you, Rosita. I'll do anything for our family."

He reached into his pocket and pulled out a worn calling card; the numbers were barely visible.

Tía's voice lit up the moment she heard us. "*Mi tía*, I have good news," I said, smiling.

"Tell me, *mi niña.*"

"We're having a baby!" Guillermo jumped in.

There was a pause. Then *tia* began to cry. We all did.

"I'm going to buy some *regalos* for the baby!" she exclaimed. "I can't wait to call Yasmine and Pedro with the good news."

Just then, a prerecorded American voice interrupted with "You have five minutes remaining."

"*Te amo, Tía. Cuídate,*" Guillermo said softly.

"*Los amo,*" she replied. "*Dios los bendiga.*"

****

As we finished the phone call, Guillermo and I found our way back to the couch and flipped through the channels until he got stuck on MTV. Billy Joel's video for "Just the Way You Are" had just begun to play.

"*Me encanta esa canción,*" he said.

With no sign of hesitation, he stood and reached for my hand, pulling me up gently. "Let's dance," he whispered softly. "*Vamos a bailar.*"

"Babe, the children are asleep, we'll wake them," I said, half-laughing.

He turned the volume up just enough for us to hear the music, so we didn't disturb the children. We were in the living room, swaying slowly, leaning into each other under the dim glow of the TV. Neither of us understood the lyrics, but somehow the song reached Guillermo in a way I couldn't explain.

After that night, every time that song came on the radio, at work, in the grocery store, anywhere, we'd start dancing right there in the middle of the aisle. I pretended to be embarrassed, but a part of me loved the attention Guillermo gave me. No matter where we were, he'd reach for my hand and ask me to dance. Even the kids caught on, their little voices calling from the next room, "Mami and Daddy, your song is on!"

Whenever I heard that song, alone at home, cleaning the salon, or folding laundry, I couldn't help but wonder if Guillermo was listening too, thinking of me at that very moment. For months, we swayed to its melody without knowing the words, guided only by the feeling it stirred in us. Then one day in class, I was assigned to study a song's lyrics. As I translated each line of Billy Joel's "Just the Way You Are," I realized how perfectly they reflected our marriage, its struggles, its tenderness, and its devotion. From that day forward, I didn't just love the song—I became a true fan of Billy Joel.

These instances, charming and unforeseen, were reminders of exactly why I loved Guillermo.

Chapter 5

"Gracia Divina"

Nearly a year into our life in New Jersey, the summer heat bore down on me day after day. On those hot days, I stocked up on cold maltas and popsicles, small comforts that made the days feel lighter. Still, my routine didn't slow down. I continued attending classes and spent a few hours each week cleaning at Carmen's salon.

By then, I was well into my second trimester, my body already adjusting to the weight of what was coming. The house we were living in felt spacious enough for our growing family.

The children had their own rooms, and we were still decorating the baby's nursery even though he would be sleeping in our room for the first several months.

Guillermo had been working late most days and had started drinking heavily again. I brought it up a few times, and though he'd stop for a few days, he always slipped back into old habits. Deep down, I knew it was only a matter of time before the cheating started again.

With him, drinking and cheating always seemed to go hand in hand, like rolling the dice and never knowing which version of him would show up.

I was scared, terrified, really. I didn't want him putting me or the baby at risk. I didn't want to catch something that no injection could cure. And with Guillermo, it felt like that shadow was creeping closer with every reckless decision.

Dios mio, I didn't even want to think about it.

Weeks had passed, and the strain in our home had begun to show. As I swept the hair from the salon floor, left behind by the stylists throughout the day, Carmen looked over and asked gently, "Are you okay? You're awfully quiet today. You seem like you've got a lot on your mind."

I looked around to make sure everyone had left.

"It's just you and me," she assured me.

"Guillermo's started drinking again," I said, my voice low. "Every night he comes home with alcohol on his breath. I've tried talking to him, but nothing's getting through." Tears began to stream down my cheeks before I could stop them.

"Don't cry," she said softly. "Have you tried talking to his best friend?"

I shook my head. "Their relationship hasn't been the same since we moved out of Alberto's rental property."

"How about your aunt?"

"No. Guillermo would be upset if I told her our problems."

"We are planning to send the kids to Miami. *Mi tía* will bring them back before I have the baby, maybe then I can talk to her about it."

"Sounds like a plan."

"Thank you for listening to me."

"Anytime, *amiga*." Carmen looked around the shop with a smile. "Well, let's get out of here."

I hated that I had shared something so personal with her. I considered Carmen a close friend, but I didn't feel comfortable telling her about my suspicion of Guillermo cheating, so I kept that to myself. I was too ashamed and embarrassed.

****

By late summer, a few weeks after that conversation with Carmen at the salon, I arrived home with a few hours to spare before Guillermo and the children returned, so I started preparing dinner, when the phone rang. Each time I answered, the caller hung up. It had been happening more often over the past weeks, and every call left a knot in my stomach. I tried to tell myself it was a wrong number, but the silence on the other end felt deliberately.

I turned the burner down and wiped my hands on the dish towel. The phone rang again. This time, I let it ring twice before answering.

"Hello?"

Silence.

I waited, heart beating in my chest.

"Who is this?" I asked, trying to sound firm.

Still, no answer. Then, just as I was about to hang up, I heard the faintest sound of someone breathing.

Chills ran down my spine.

"If this is some kind of joke, it's not funny," I said, slamming the phone down.

I stood there for a moment, staring at the wall, trying to shake this uneasiness. I didn't want to confront Guillermo. Not yet. But something told me this wasn't over.

****

Guillermo and the children walked in, the kids laughing and talking over one another as they rushed to tell me about their day. I smiled and tried to take it all in, but my eyes drifted to Guillermo. Something about him seemed…off. His smile didn't quite reach his eyes.

"Okay, time for baths," I said, gently nudging the kids down the hallway. "And don't forget your homework."

Guillermo came over, kissed me on the cheek, and placed a warm hand on my belly. "How's my baby?"

"We're fine," I said softly. "What about you? Is everything okay?"

"Just a long day," he said, brushing past the question.

The phone rang, and I instinctively looked over at him. Without hesitation, he picked it up and stepped into the living room. The kids were playing and the TV was up, so I couldn't make out what he was saying. His tone was low, careful. The call didn't last long.

When he came back, I casually asked, "Who was that?"

"A co-worker. He needs a ride in the morning."

I nodded. "How's work?"

He sighed. "I've been busting my ass, taking on more responsibilities, coming up with plans. That's good, right?"

"It is," I said, watching him. "Has Alberto mentioned a raise?"

"I brought it up once," Guillermo said. "Alberto told me he'd have to review the budget." He hesitated. "I told him there's another mouth to feed soon."

"Hopefully, he'll realize what you're worth and give you that raise," I said, trying to keep the conversation light.

"How's class going?"

"I've got one more English class left. After that, I can apply for the nursing program. I hear they might accept my coursework from Cuba, which means I'd have fewer course classes before I can take the licensing exam."

He smiled. "I'm so proud of you."

"Thank you, baby."

Just then, the kids came running into the kitchen. "Mami, we're hungry!"

"Alright, alright, go sit down. I'm serving dinner now."

We gathered around the table, and while we ate and chatted, I kept watching Guillermo, studying his face, wondering what he wasn't saying. I prayed, truly prayed that whatever demons he carried, he had buried them in Cuba. Because if I found out he was cheating again, neither the kids nor I would be staying around. Not this time.

****

The kids spotted the golden arches in the distance and immediately started pointing and shouting, "We want a Happy Meal!" I knew it wasn't just the cheeseburgers they were after. It was the toy tucked inside that little box. Watching them made me smile. I was so proud of how well they were adjusting to life in America. I often asked if they missed Cuba, and every time, they shook their heads and said no, they liked it better here. I always reminded them to never forget where they came from. While we may live in America, Cuba is where we are from.

As we sat and ate, I found myself in happy tears. They were like two little versions of Guillermo and me, full of life, energy, and wonder. Time was flying by so quickly. I was so proud of them both. They were doing so well in school.

Then Isabelle walked in with her kids. My children rushed over to invite them to sit with us, their excitement spilling into the space between us. It was awkward, knowing our husbands were having some issues at work. Still, Isabelle had always been a loyal friend, kind, supportive, and genuine.

"Wow, look at your stomach.

"I'm halfway there," I said, unable to hide my excitement.

Isabelle looked heavier than the last time I saw her, and I could relate. The food here in America is overly processed, loaded with glucose, preservatives, and additives. I thought about all this while enjoying a large fry with extra salt. And between the kids and the husbands, finding time for yourself wasn't easy.

We started talking about Cuba when she suddenly asked, "How's Guillermo's dad doing?"

I froze. "Why do you ask?"

"I heard he's very ill."

The words sank in slowly, then hit all at once. My throat tightened, and before I could stop myself, the tears came.

"I'm so sorry," she said, clearly surprised. "I thought you knew."

"No," I whispered. "I had no idea."

A heaviness settled over me. Why wouldn't Guillermo tell me something like this? Why keep it from me?

An awkward silence grew between us until Isabelle finally blurted,

"I'd really like to host your baby shower."

I nodded, still trying to steady my emotions. "That's kind of you. Thank you. I think Carmen mentioned wanting to do something, too. I'll connect you both."

We talked for a few more minutes, then after Isabelle left, I sat in silence.

Guillermo's drinking, the distance in his eyes, the way he seemed lost in thought lately, it all made sense now. He was worried about his father. But why not come to me? Why carry that alone?

And why did I feel like, once again, I was the last to know what was going on in my own marriage?

****

When we arrived home, Guillermo was passed out on the couch, fast asleep, with our wood panel floor model TV watching him. The kids ran over, proudly showing off their toys from McDonald's.

"Papi! Papi, look!" they shouted. "Look what we got!"

"*Qué lindo*," he murmured with a tired smile, still half-asleep. "It's nap time. Go in your room and let Papi rest."

I sat down beside him and gently caressed his face. "How was work today?" I asked, leaning in to kiss him softly.

"It was too long a day without you by my side," he said, his voice low and full of warmth.

I stood and gave him a playful smile. "Let's go in the room so you can show me just how much you missed me."

Guillermo stood too, rubbing my backside as I walked ahead. "Look at that wagon," he whispered. "*Coño.*"

I laughed, looking back at him. "Guillermo…"

He pointed down to the growing bulge in his pants. "You see what you do to me?"

He reached for my hand, and together we walked to the bedroom. He closed the door gently behind us, then began undressing me, piece by piece. His mouth found my nipples warm, slow, and patient as he lay me back and placed a pillow beneath my head. Then, he kissed his way down between my thighs, his touch deliberate, his breath warm against my skin.

Our bodies moved in rhythm, the space between us melting away as I whispered his name. He turned me to my side, pressing close, and slipped inside me. It wasn't just physical, it was something we both needed. A way to feel close again. A way to remember who we were before the weight of everything else.

Afterward, as we lay tangled together in bed, my mind drifted to my conversation with Isabelle. Guillermo's father. His illness. The silence between us suddenly felt heavier. I wanted so badly to ask him about it, to understand what he was carrying, but I was afraid. Afraid it might change the mood, or open a wound he wasn't ready to share. So I stayed still, holding him close, and let the moment last a little longer.

I traced circles on Guillermo's chest with my fingertip, listening to the steady rhythm of his breath. He looked peaceful, like a man finally at ease. But I wasn't.

The room was still, the kind of quiet that made your thoughts louder. My conversation with Isabelle kept replaying in my mind, her voice and the way she hesitated before telling me about his father. I couldn't shake the feeling that I should have known. That he should've told me.

I wanted to ask him. Right then. Just whisper the question into the stillness between us and let the truth land where it may. But I didn't. I couldn't.

Maybe I was afraid of the answer. Or maybe I didn't want to ruin the softness of the moment, the first moment of connection we'd had in days. I didn't want his guilt or grief to harden the tenderness we'd just shared. And I definitely didn't want him to shut down, the way he sometimes did when things got too heavy.

So instead, I lay there and held him. I listened to the hum of the air conditioner, the occasional honk of a car horn outside, the bachata music playing in the distance, a few doors down, the creak of the bed as he shifted slightly in his sleep. And I told myself I'd ask tomorrow, but just not today.

The next morning, I woke up before the sun. The house was still, the kind of stillness that feels sacred in a home with children. I moved quietly, careful not to wake anyone, and made my way to the kitchen.

I stood at the stove, scrambling eggs and frying slices of plátano maduro and *salchichas*, trying to keep my hands busy while my mind wandered. Guillermo hadn't stirred. He'd fallen asleep with his arm around me, but now he was snoring gently, wrapped in the sheets like nothing in the world was weighing on him.

Maybe it wasn't. Maybe he'd found a way to keep it all tucked inside, sealed off where no one could touch it, not even me.

The coffee finished brewing, filling the kitchen with its warm, earthy aroma. I poured two cups and set one on the table for him. I bought a fresh roll of Pan Cubano from the bodega and toasted the bread with butter.

I knew I needed to talk to him. I told myself I would. But as the minutes passed and the light outside shifted from deep blue to gold, I felt the knot in my chest tighten.

Guillermo came into the kitchen a little while later, stretching and rubbing his eyes.

"Smells good in here," he said, planting a kiss on my cheek.

"*El café está en la mesa*," I replied, keeping my tone even.

He sat down, took a sip, and let out a satisfied sigh. "*Perfecto, como siempre.*"

I smiled faintly but didn't respond.

He didn't ask what was wrong, and I didn't offer. He talked about work, about the guys on the job site, about maybe asking Alberto again for that raise. I nodded in the right places, smiled where it was expected. But inside, the silence grew between us and in me. I kept thinking: what else hasn't he told me?

By the time the kids wandered into the kitchen, rubbing their eyes and asking what was for breakfast, the moment had already slipped away. The phone rang, and I picked it up. An operator from Cuba asked if we would accept a call. Guillermo jumped up at the mention of Cuba, digging through his pockets for a few worn calling cards.

"Tell them we'll call back," he said urgently, almost out of breath.

I relayed the message to the operator, knowing the person on the other end could probably hear me. Calls from Cuba were always complicated and expensive, usually routed through a third-party service. Sometimes the connection was terrible, and they called multiple times until they got through.

One minute could cost nearly $35. Calling back with a card was cheaper, but even then, a $10 card barely gave us ten minutes.

Still, those calls always made my heart race. You never knew what news was waiting on the other end—good or bad.

Guillermo went into the bedroom to return the call. I turned off the stove and was checking on the kids when I suddenly heard him crying. I rushed to the room, heart pounding.

"*Mi papá... Mi papá... Se murió*," he sobbed, collapsing into my arms. Guillermo held me and wept like a child. I gently took the phone from his hand. It had already gone silent. The call was over.

I urged him to lie down, though my own legs felt unsteady beneath me. I couldn't believe Guillo was gone. He was more than Guillermo's father—he was like a father to me, too. He always looked after the kids whenever we needed help. Honestly, he was part of the reason Guillermo and I were still together.

Guillo didn't tolerate nonsense. He was firm, principled, and wanted better for his son. His mother was from the Canary Islands, off the coast of Spain, and his father had come to Cuba from Saint Kitts in the western Antilles. Guillo raised Guillermo on his own and demanded respect not just from others, but from life itself.

I called Alberto to let him know that Guillo had passed. As soon as I said the words, his voice cracked.

"*Ay no... Guillo?*" he whispered, choking back tears. "He was a good man. I'm so sorry, *mi hermana*."

He took a moment to gather himself before continuing. "Listen, don't worry about the kids. Isabelle will come by in the morning and take them to school. And tell Guillermo not to even think about work. I'm giving him the rest of the week off with pay."

"Thank you, Alberto," I said softly. "That means a lot."

"Of course. You all are family."

I hung up and called Carmen next. As soon as she heard the news, she didn't hesitate. "I'll be there," she said. "I'll bring over food tomorrow and some extra for the freezer, too. Y'all shouldn't have to lift a finger."

I called *mi tía*, and without hesitation, she mailed us a check. I told her we didn't need it, but the more I tried to decline, the more offended she became.

"You are my niece," she said firmly. "And as long as I'm breathing, I'm going to support you."

Shortly after, Yasmine called too. "Whatever you need, just say the word," she offered.

We agreed to receive visitors starting on Thursday of that week. It felt like the right time, with enough space to catch our breath, and close enough to feel the love of those who cherished Guillo most.

By then, our home was filled with the comforting hum of voices, the clatter of dishes, and the rich, familiar scents of home-cooked meals. Friends and neighbors came bearing trays of arroz con pollo, sweet plantains, tamales, and flan. Carmen set up a long folding table in the backyard, and Isabelle brought extra chairs from her church.

But it wasn't just food, it was love. For the first time, I felt like America, like Paterson, New Jersey, was home. Our village showed up for us in every way. They hugged us, prayed with us, and laughed through their tears, sharing memories of Guillo. How he'd sit on the porch sipping *cafecito*, shouting advice to the neighborhood kids like he was the community elder. And the truth was, he was just that.

In that moment, I realized just how blessed we were. Even in our grief, our community wrapped itself around us. They didn't wait to be asked; they simply showed up. That's the thing about real friends and chosen family: when one of us hurts, we all feel it. And somehow, in that togetherness, healing quietly begins.

Later that evening, I asked Guillermo to promise me he would never keep anything from me again, that we were partners for life. He told me he didn't want to worry me, since I was pregnant. Then he nodded, his eyes heavy with emotion, and said he'd slow down on the drinking too.

And through it all, I was grateful that he and Alberto were finally on better terms. There was peace between them now, something I know Guillo would have wanted.

That night, we lit a candle, thanking God for Guillo and prayed that he was finally at peace. Still, anxiety settled in me, I knew deep down inside, I was carrying more than a child, I was carrying doubt, fear, and the weight of knowing something was about to change.

Chapter 6

Tuya y Mas Que Tuya

In the weeks that followed, the unease I'd been carrying began to take shape. The kids were heading to Miami to spend the rest of the summer with *mi tía*. Yasmine assured me they'd be fine flying alone. She said the flight attendants would keep a close eye on them. I'd never even been on a plane myself, so I was a nervous wreck. I wrote little notes with hearts all over them, and words that would remind the kids how much their dad and I loved them, and they are a blessing from God. I pinned a note to both of their shirts, just in case, and tucked another into each of their book bags. Before they left, I reminded them to be on their best behavior.

"I don't want you giving *Tia* any trouble, okay? You hear me?"

"Yes, Mami," they chimed in unison.

I packed their favorite snacks and clothes, and we even stopped by McDonald's on the way to the airport. Surprisingly, Guillermo was okay with them flying without us. I think seeing how excited they were made it easier for him. As we walked toward the gate, I couldn't hold back my tears.

Yasmine had promised to take them to Disney World, and that's all they could talk about: Mickey Mouse this, Mickey Mouse that. Watching them go, all grown up with their little backpacks and matching outfits, was surreal. I kept it together until they boarded, but once that plane took off, my heart ached. I was really going to miss my babies.

That's when Guillermo turned to me with a sly smile and said he had a surprise.

"Vamos a Nueva York."

"¿Tú estás loco?" I laughed. *"Vamos…"*

The next day, we hit the road for New York City, our first time. Along the way, we picked up pizza and sodas, and when we finally got there, it was everything I had imagined. The tall buildings, the fast pace, the honking of car horns, people from every background rushing by… I was in awe. It felt like I was in a movie, and Guillermo was my leading man.

We didn't stay long, though. We knew Tía would be calling soon, so off we were back to Paterson, which was more than an hour and a half ride back. The trip had been wonderful and way too short. I'd wanted to ride on the subway, visit the Statue of Liberty and the Empire State Building. We had to come back with the kids.

I dozed off as we drove through the city, lulled by the hum of the car and the rhythm of the road. Just as I was drifting, our song came on the radio. Guillermo started singing to me in his charming, broken English, serenading me long after the song had ended. Then he switched the station, and salsa music filled the car, pulsing through the speakers the rest of the way home. I was so tired and eager to get to bed, but not without talking to my children.

Soon after we arrived home, we called *mi tía*, and the kids had arrived safely. She handed them the phone.

"Mami, we saw the sky," Antonio said, "but we didn't see Guillo.

"He's with God," I said.

Guillermo choked up a little. Then he told them to behave and that he had a surprise waiting for them when they got back.

"Okay, bye Mami, bye Papi. *Un besito. Cuídate.*"

I could tell Guillermo was missing them already, and after a quiet dinner, he crashed on the couch.

****

It was a balmy Monday. The salon was quiet that afternoon. Only one appointment on the books, and the customer canceled at the last minute. I stayed anyway. There was something comforting about being there, sweeping up stray hairs, organizing the polish rack, and folding towels. It gave me a sense of purpose. Plus, we needed the money. With the kids gone for the summer, Guillermo and I agreed to pick up extra hours wherever we could. With the baby coming soon, we could use the extra funds. But more than anything, I needed the distraction.

The silence at home felt strange, almost hollow. After tidying up the kids' room and the nursery, it hit me that so much of my identity was wrapped up in being a mother and a wife. Outside of them, I didn't have much that belonged to me. That's when I realized how much I missed being in school, and how much I missed learning and growing. Needless to say, cleaning the salon had become my only social outlet, a place where I could feel like myself again.

Carmen sat at her station, combing her hair in the mirror, humming softly.

"You ever think about going back to school?" I asked suddenly.

She turned, a little surprised. "You?"

I nodded. "I have one more English class to finish. Then I can apply to the nursing program. I miss learning. I miss doing something that's just for me."

"I think that's beautiful," she said. "You'd make a great nurse, Ro. You already take care of everybody else."

I smiled and sat across from her. "What about you? Ever think about doing something else?"

She shrugged. "I like it here. I love helping women feel good about themselves. Plus, Maya and I are saving up. We're hoping to open our own little restaurant one day."

"Maya?" I tilted my head, teasing. "Who is Maya? Have I met her already?"

Carmen chuckled. "No, you haven't."

"Well, now I'm asking. *¿Quién es Maya?*

She smiled, soft and sure. "Maya's my girlfriend. We've been together for two years this spring. She's a chef and runs the kitchen at that little Cuban spot on Broad Street."

Carmen handed me a photo. Maya was a blue-eyed *gringa* from Massachusetts. Blonde and fair-skinned—the last thing I expected.

I blinked a few times, more surprised than anything. Not wanting to offend her, I offered a smile. "That's Maya? I've eaten there. Her *congri* is delicious."

Carmen leaned back in her chair, pride lighting up her face. "She'll love hearing that."

There was a pause between us, not tense, just awkward.

Suddenly, so many things about her relationship with her children's father made sense. All the things she hadn't said before, now quietly filled in. Now, I could see it. The way she walked and talked was somewhat masculine. She rarely wore makeup. Even the way she wore her hair seemed masculine to me.

"I hope I'm not making you uncomfortable," Carmen said gently.

"No, not at all," I replied. And I meant it.

Carmen raised an eyebrow. "You sure?"

I nodded. "I mean… It must feel good. To have someone who sees you. All of you."

She didn't say anything right away. She just reached out and touched my hand.

"You deserve that too, Rosita. Not just love, but a life that feels whole. One that you choose, not one that just happens to you."

I laughed softly, a little embarrassed. I looked directly at her.

"Guillermo can be a pain in the butt sometimes, but I wouldn't trade him for anything in the world. I love Guillermo. I love him even though he's not perfect."

She smiled and nodded. "I hear you, loud and clear, Ro."

"Speaking of which," I said, looking at the clock, "I should probably get going. He'll be home soon."

"Do you want a ride?"

"No, no, that's okay. I'll hop on the bus."

"You sure?"

"Yeah. I'll see you on Wednesday."

Carmen gave me a quick hug before I grabbed my bag and headed out.

As I stepped out into the warm evening air, a small crowd had gathered in front of the bodega, men talking loudly, laughing between sips of beer and whatever else. A group of kids zipped past on their bikes, weaving through the sidewalk, eager to break free from the crowd blocking their path.

I crossed the street just in time. The city bus pulled up with a soft groan, and the door swung open with a hiss. The bus was fairly crowded, and there were a few empty seats upfront across from the driver.

I took a seat near the front and stared out the window as the city drifted by, a blur of lights and motion. Soft conversations rose and fell around me, but I couldn't focus on any of them. My mind was elsewhere, replaying Carmen's words over and over. I just couldn't shake them.

You deserve that too, Rosita.

Her words lingered in my mind like a melody I wasn't quite ready to hear.

My life was whole and complete. It would be nice to have more money in my pocket, but money couldn't keep me warm at night or give me the feeling of being loved the way Guillermo did for me.

But then another thought crept in: one I didn't want to admit.

I wasn't sure how Guillermo would react if he knew Carmen was gay.

He liked Carmen. Always respected her hustle. But this? I wasn't sure. He could be old-fashioned about certain things— things he didn't understand. Things that made him uncomfortable. And even though he had softened a bit over the years, I still knew the look he gave when something didn't sit right with him.

Part of me wanted to protect Carmen. The other part didn't want to deal with the argument that might follow. What if he didn't want me working there anymore? What if he started asking questions, making assumptions?

I sighed and shifted my bag on my shoulder. Carmen had trusted me with something personal, something sacred. That meant something. I wasn't about to go home and treat it like gossip. It wasn't mine to explain; it was hers to live. So, I decided I wouldn't say anything. Not now. Not unless it mattered.

And if it ever did, I'd find the right words to tell him. He can't choose my friends. I may not understand her physical attraction to women, but she had been good to me, and that was all that mattered.

As I was opening the door, Guillermo crept up behind me. I jumped, and he hugged me and kissed me on the cheek. He scared the daylights out of me.

****

Guillermo was sitting on the couch, flipping through channels, a plate of picadillo con arroz balanced on his lap. A bottle of *malta* stood on the side of the couch. I was folding laundry at the table, humming to myself, feeling the kind of peace that only came after a long day.

"You said Carmen's girl works at that Cuban spot on Broad Street, right?" he asked casually.

I froze for just a second, then nodded. "Yeah…Maya. Why?"

He shrugged. "I was talking to Enrique at work. He said his cousin works there too. She mentioned Carmen and Maya are…together."

I paused, choosing my words carefully. "They are."

Guillermo blinked, slowly turning toward me. "Together like…*novias*?"

I nodded again. "Yes. They've been together for two years."

He stared at the TV, but he wasn't watching it. I knew that look. Something was brewing in his thoughts.

"You knew?" he asked.

"I did," I said, folding a towel and setting it aside. "She told me last week."

He leaned back, rubbing his chin. "Huh."

A long silence stretched between us. I could feel him trying to wrap his mind around it.

"She's still the same Carmen," I said softly. "She's kind. She's honest. She's good to me. None of that has changed."

"I didn't say she wasn't."

I sat across from him. "But you're thinking about it."

He met my eyes, the hesitation clear. "It's just…I wasn't expecting that."

"Well, life doesn't always give you warnings," I said, gently but firmly. "She trusted me with it. And I trust her. That's all that matters."

He stared at me for a long time before speaking. "You still gonna keep working there?"

"*Si, claro.*" Who she chooses to love should not matter to our friendship or our working relationship.

Guillermo sighed and shook his head slightly. "I guess it's not my business. She's always been good to you. And if she's happy, then...*bueno.*"

I smiled. "She is."

He nodded and picked up his fork again. "As long as she ain't trying to hit on you."

I rolled my eyes. *"Ay, por favor."*

He grinned and winked. "I'm just saying. You're still fine as hell, pregnant and all, Rosita."

I tossed a balled up sock at him, and he threw it back at me. We both broke into laughter. Guillermo always found a way to surprise me. Just when I thought I knew where he was headed, he'd take a turn in an entirely different direction. That was Guillermo—unpredictable, in the most unexpected ways.

Chapter 7

"Yo Viviré"

By the time fall arrived, we had been back together as a family, and my pregnancy had begun to show in ways I could no longer ignore. I was deep into my third trimester, exhausted and more than ready to have this baby. "Any day now," my doctor had said. My belly had grown so large I could barely see my feet, and getting up felt like a full-body workout.

And this pregnancy felt different from the others. My stomach was noticeably larger, and the baby seemed to rest right on my bladder, making even the simplest tasks uncomfortable. I was so swollen and tired that I couldn't even enjoy our first snowfall with Guillermo and the kids.

They went outside without me, bundled up and laughed, and built a snowman in the front yard. By the next morning, the kids noticed the head had been knocked off, but they still came inside beaming, cheeks rosy, full of stories about their snowy adventure. It was early winter by then, and for the kids, Christmas already felt close.

"*¿Cuándo* viene Santa Claus?" they asked eagerly. This *viejo blanco con un bigote*, they'd learned about in school, the one who was supposed to bring gifts down a chimney we didn't even have.

Just one more thing to add to the growing mountain of things we had to figure out. Good thing, Christmas was still some time away. My focus, for now, was on a different kind of arrival: the baby growing heavier with each passing day.

Guillermo joked that the baby would arrive when it turned eighteen. I was starting to believe him until one morning, just after breakfast, my water broke.

I called Guillermo at work, but the receptionist kept putting me on hold. When she finally came back, she told me he had already left for the day. My heart sank. Where could he be? Surely, he must be on his way home, but this baby isn't waiting for anyone. I immediately called Isabelle, and without hesitation, she offered to take me to the hospital.

Everything was ready, my overnight bag was packed, the baby's clothes were neatly folded in a small duffel, and my hospital papers were tucked in a folder by the door. Isabelle arrived in under ten minutes, breathless and concerned. She helped me down the steps and into her car as I breathed through the slow, steady contractions.

When we arrived at the hospital, the contractions were coming every seven minutes. The nurses admitted me quickly, and as they settled me into a room, I kept glancing at the door, hoping Guillermo would walk through it. But an hour passed, and there was still no sign of him. This wasn't like him, and I was starting to worry.

"I'm going to call Alberto," Isabelle said softly, brushing a strand of hair from my damp forehead.

"Please," I whispered, trying to hide the disappointment in my voice.

At that moment, I realized the baby might arrive before Guillermo even knew I was in labor. But I also knew I was strong and I wasn't alone.

Then, suddenly, the door burst open and Guillermo rushed in, drenched in sweat. He hugged Isabelle tightly, thanking her for bringing me to the hospital.

"*Mi vida, lo siento*," he said, breathlessly. "I was at the construction site when my coworker came running to tell me you were in labor. I got here as fast as I could."

That's strange, I thought. The secretary said he had left for the day.

But my contractions were intensifying by the minute, and all I could focus on was bringing our baby into the world. Guillermo squeezed my hand and smiled. I closed my eyes, matching my breath to a steady rhythm. Our baby was on the way.

"Push," the doctor said. Then again, "Push."

And just like that, I heard the sweetest sound—our baby crying.

"It's a girl," the doctor announced.

Guillermo cut the umbilical cord, and moments later, they placed her in my arms. I couldn't stop crying. Guillermo kissed my forehead and whispered, "Our daughter is here." The days that followed passed in a blur of feedings, visitors, and sleepless nights.

Carolina was beautiful, with a head full of hair and big, curious eyes. When I looked into them, I saw nothing but greatness, just as I had with my other children. We named her Carolina María Martínez, after *mi tía*.

When we called *mi tia*, she went silent and began to cry.

"*No llores, tia*," I said gently. "You've been so good to us."

I had already spoken to Yasmine and Pedro, and they agreed to be Carolina's godparents.

****

We had so many visitors that came to the hospital and at our home: Carmen and Maya, Alberto and Isabelle, all arriving with gifts in tow. *Mi tía* returned to New Jersey shortly after I gave birth and stayed with us for several weeks.

She was a tremendous help. At night, she would stay up with the baby while Guillermo and I slept. Carolina was a good baby: she rarely cried, except when it was time to breastfeed.

Mi tía took us shopping and insisted on buying us a newer used car, a red station wagon. *"Es tiempo, mi hijo,"* Tia said. We appreciated the gift and kept the other car for me so I wouldn't have to take the bus with the baby.

With everything that had happened in the past few months, including the death of Guillo and the birth of Carolina, having *mi tia* around was truly a blessing.

Our days quickly fell into a rhythm. The kids and the baby were on a tight schedule, and by 7:30 p.m., they were in bed. Paterson, New Jersey, was beginning to feel like home. And although we had people in our lives who felt like family, when it came time for *tia* to leave, we were all sad to see her go.

****

Outside of our little cocoon of new baby bliss, the world was changing at a speeding rate and not for the better. Reaganomics was in full swing, and it was kicking our butts. Programs were being cut left and right. Free lunch at school was no longer guaranteed, and food stamps had become harder to qualify for. Everything felt like it was shrinking except the bills. Guillermo started bracing for layoffs, and we were all holding our breath. Feeding a family of five in this new America meant stretching every dollar and making do with less. Groceries cost more, gas prices crept up, and the jobs that once seemed steady no longer felt secure. The dream we had crossed the ocean for was still alive, but it now came with a price tag and fewer safety nets to catch us when we stumbled. Though times were often tough, we were blessed to call America home.

Guillermo started picking up extra shifts wherever he could: weekend construction jobs, roofing gigs, even hauling furniture for a moving company when needed. He came home every night sore and silent, his hands rougher than they used to be. I began babysitting for neighbors, anything to bring in a few extra dollars. We clipped coupons, bought in bulk when we could, and stretched every meal with rice and beans. *La caja de queso* that the government was handing out was *riquísimo*, but it wasn't enough. Sometimes, I'd lie awake at night doing the math in my head, counting diapers, school supplies, and grocery lists against what we had in the bank.

We weren't alone, and everyone we knew was hustling to survive. Isabelle started cleaning houses in nearby neighborhoods, and Carmen was trying to keep her salon afloat by offering discounts to loyal clients. The women in our community leaned on each other, swapping meals, sharing hand-me-downs, and watching each other's kids after school.

Mi tía often reminded me: "*Esta no es la America de tus abuelos*, but you still have to find a way." And we did. Somehow, we did.

Though the promise of America hadn't disappeared, it just demanded more grit than we had imagined. And even when the government tightened its grip, we held on to each other, because that, at least, cost nothing.

****

By the time Carolina was starting to crawl, nearly a year had passed since her birth. The older kids were growing fast, asking for bigger things we simply couldn't afford. I had to postpone my

English class until the new year, and while life kept moving forward, I could sense something changing in Guillermo.

The long hours, the pressure of providing, the weight of this American life, it was all starting to wear him down. Slowly, almost imperceptibly, he began drinking again. First, a beer after work, then rum on the weekends, and before long, the smell of alcohol was back on his breath almost daily.

He promised it was just to take the pressure off. That he was fine. That he was in control. But I knew better. I'd seen this pattern before.

The late nights returned. So did the vague explanations and the smell of perfume that wasn't mine. He stopped looking me in the eye when he came home, and the house phone was always within arm's reach of him, something he never used to do. My heart sank the night I found a receipt for two mojitos and an appetizer from a Cuban café nowhere near any of his job sites.

And then came a woman I'd heard him mention once or twice, Sandra, I think. She worked with him on the roofing crew, helping with scheduling and materials, he'd said. He spoke of her casually, too casually, but his tone gave him away. The way he said her name had a softness to it that didn't belong to work talk.

I didn't say anything at first. I watched. I waited. I folded his laundry and looked for lipstick, and checked for the scent of perfume. I listened for changes in his voice when he answered his phone, and at night, when he rolled over in bed without touching me, I stared at the ceiling, wondering if the man beside me still saw me or if someone else had taken my place in his mind.

I wondered what she looked like. Was she *una rubia?* Did she speak with fancy words, wear elegant clothes, and have *un cuerpaso?* Did she have more to offer him than me and the kids? *Dios mío*, who holds his heart?

The house felt heavy with secrets. I wasn't ready to confront them yet, but the storm was coming.

****

I didn't tell *mi tía* right away. She had just left, and I didn't want to worry her, or worse, hear the disappointment in her voice. But Carmen noticed something.

We were sitting outside her salon one afternoon, watching the kids ride their bikes up and down the sidewalk, when she asked gently, "You okay, *mija*? You've been quiet lately. Real quiet."

I hesitated. Then I shrugged. "Just tired."

She didn't press, just nodded and handed me a cold soda. But later, when we were sweeping up inside, she tried again. "I don't want to get in your business, Rosita, but I've seen that look before. You don't have to say much, just know I'm here."

That's when the words started to form slowly and unsure. "Guillermo's been…different lately. Distant. And I think…" I paused, struggling to say it aloud. "I think there might be someone else."

Carmen didn't gasp. She didn't look surprised. She just stopped sweeping and leaned the broom against the wall. "Is she someone you know?"

I shook my head. "He says she works with him. Sandra. I don't have proof, but my gut won't stop whispering."

Carmen stepped closer, her voice low but steady. "Listen to your gut. It never lies. But don't let it eat you alive either. You've been through too much to carry this all by yourself."

I nodded, blinking back tears. "I don't want to believe it, Carmen. After everything we've been through…"

"I know," she said. "But whether it's true or not, you deserve honesty. And peace."

****

That night, I watched Guillermo fall asleep on the couch, half a beer in his hand, the TV still on. I covered him with a blanket, picked up Carolina, and tiptoed to the bedroom alone, my mind already thinking about the question I didn't yet have the courage to ask: What do you do when the dream you fought for starts to crumble?

But something in me shifted. I was done pretending not to see what was in front of me.

After putting the baby to sleep, I walked back into the living room and gently shook Guillermo awake.

"Guillermo," I said, barely above a whisper. "Wake up."

He stirred, groggy, rubbing his eyes. "Huh? What time is it?"

"*No importa*," I snapped.

He blinked, looking confused. "*¿Cómo?*"

I stared at him, my voice steady now. "*¿Quién es ella?*"

He sat up slowly, the weight of my question settling over him like a boulder. He didn't answer right away, just looked at me, his face tight, unreadable.

"I don't know what you're talking about," he said finally, voice low.

"Don't lie to me, Guillermo," I said, folding my arms. "The long hours, the smell of perfume, the way you guard the house phone. I left Cuba with you, not to be disrespected."

His jaw clenched. "There's no one else."

"Then say her name," I challenged. "Say it. Sandra."

He froze.

That silence was louder than any confession. My throat tightened. I didn't cry. Not this time.

"You swore things would be different here," I whispered. "You promised our family would come first."

He lowered his head, resting his elbows on his knees, hands clasped. "I didn't mean for it to happen."

"But it did. And now I have to decide what happens next."

The baby woke up in the next room, a soft whimper breaking the silence.

"I need you to leave," I said. "No sleeping in our bed tonight."

He looked up at me, guilt and fear in his eyes. "Rosita—"

"I'm not asking," I said, turning away.

As I walked down the hallway, I didn't feel triumphant. I felt tired. I also felt something I hadn't felt in a long time—clarity.

He gathered his stuff and left.

The dream may have cracked in pieces, but I was still standing. And so were my children. And somewhere deep inside me, I knew I'd survive this too.

Chapter 8

"Tu Voz"

The emptiness I'd been carrying was heavier than I imagined. I missed Guillermo more than I wanted to admit. His touch, his voice, even the quiet moments spent between us. I also knew that letting him back in would be an invitation to more of the same. He would stray again. As much as I ached for him, I held firm. I couldn't model that kind of love for my children. I refused to show them that betrayal was something you simply learned to live with.

The kids had questions, of course, they did. It had been weeks since Guillermo left, and the silence he left behind was louder than anything imagined. I couldn't believe he had not been by to see them since he left. Knowing Guillermo, he is too ashamed to show his face.

One evening, we were cleaning up after dinner when Karime asked, her voice barely above a whisper, "Is Papi coming back?"

I paused, frozen with a dish in my hand, the words caught in my throat. Even Carolina became fussy in her high chair as though she expected a different response.

Before I could answer, Antonio pushed his plate away and looked at me with wide, wet eyes. "He's never coming back to live with us, is he?"

My heart cracked open right there at the kitchen table. I walked over and knelt beside him, pulling him into my arms. "*Mijo…*" I began searching for the truth that wouldn't shatter him completely. "Papi loves you. He loves both of you so much. But sometimes…even when people love each other, they need to live in different places."

Antonio held on to me with his little body trembling. "He doesn't love me anymore?"

I took a breath, holding back my own tears. "Things between Papi and me got complicated. It doesn't mean you did anything wrong. And it doesn't mean he loves you any less. He's still your father. That will never change."

After I tucked the kids into bed, I slipped into the kitchen, phone in hand, and called *mi tía*. She answered on the second ring, her voice instantly warm.

"*¡Mi niña! Qué alegría escucharte,*" she said, the usual joy spilling through the line.

I smiled, but it faded quickly. I hadn't said much yet, but it didn't take her long to hear the pain in my voice and detect that something was off.

"*¿Qué pasó, mi vida?*" she asked gently.

I hesitated, my eyes welling up before I could stop them. "Guillermo moved out," I said, the words feeling heavier out loud than they did in my head.

A pause. Then a soft sigh. "*Ay, mi amor…lo sabía.* I could feel something in my bones. Are you okay?"

"I'm trying to be. The kids…" I stopped, swallowing the lump in my throat. "They keep asking if he's coming back."

"And what do you say?"

"I tell them he loves them. That we're still a family…just different now."

She didn't speak for a moment, letting the silence set in. "You're strong, Rosita. But you don't have to carry this alone. Do you hear me?"

I nodded, wiping my eyes. "I hear you."

"Good. Because no matter what happens with Guillermo, *tú no estás sola*. I'm here. Always," she said. Then her tone shifted slightly. "How are you doing with money?"

I hesitated. "The bills are paid this month, but I'm not sure about next month. I've been thinking about moving into a smaller place, maybe an apartment. I don't want the kids to have to switch schools. The kids love their school. I have an appointment at the welfare office to apply for food stamps. I should qualify."

Without missing a beat, she said, "I'm going to pay your rent for a few months just until you get back on your feet."

"*Ay*, Tía…you're doing too much. I know you're on a fixed income."

"*No me importa*. Don't worry about me."

Her voice wrapped around me like a warm blanket. And at that moment, even though I was sitting alone in the kitchen, I didn't feel quite so alone.

As I lay in bed later that night, trying to quiet my thoughts, I heard the soft shuffle of feet just outside my bedroom door. Antonio peeked in first, clutching his pillow. Without a word, he climbed into bed beside me, nestling close like he used to when he was little. A few minutes later, Karime tiptoed in and curled up on my other side. They hadn't done this in years. My three babies lying beside me reminded me how blessed I was.

The separation was clearly affecting them more than they let on, especially Antonio. I just wrapped an arm around each of them and held them close.

Earlier that week, I'd received a call from his teacher. "Hi, Ms. Martínez," she began, her voice careful. "I wanted to check in with you about Antonio. He's been acting out a bit in class, talking back, not focusing, even getting into little arguments with the other kids."

I sighed, already expecting the call. "We're going through a tough time at home," I said gently. "His father and I are separated."

"Oh," she said quietly, "I'm sorry to hear that."

"I didn't want to get into the details with him," I added, "but I know it's been weighing on him. I'll talk to him. Thank you for letting me know."

Now, lying there with both of them wrapped around me, I could feel how much they needed me and how much they missed their father. I stroked Antonio's hair gently, and he reached for my hand.

"Are we gonna be okay, Mami?" he asked, his voice barely a whisper.

"Yes, *mi amor*," I whispered back, kissing the top of his head. "We're going to be just fine."

And in that moment, even with everything uncertain, I finally believed my own words.

****

After running a few errands, I decided to stop by the school to visit my teacher, Ms. Susan Roth. She was a petite white woman with rimmed glasses and long, reddish-brown hair that reached down to her lower back. She wore quirky clothes and chunky jewelry. Everything about her was a statement. She was a walking billboard. She called herself a *feminista*.

"You know," she said one day in class after a long pause, "people always think feminism is about marching or shouting. But sometimes, it's just about showing up for yourself when no one else will. Choosing your future even when it's hard."

Those words stayed with me. It felt like I had been fighting for myself for a long time, long before I even knew what to call it. That's how we connected. She saw that in me. And maybe, for the first time, I saw it in myself too.

When she saw me walk in, her face lit up.

"Rosa! What a lovely surprise," she said, stepping out from behind her desk. "Come in, sit down. How have you been?"

It didn't take much for the tears to start. As soon as I stepped into her office, I broke down. I missed class more than I realized, and suddenly it all came pouring out.

"I've been going through a lot," I confessed. "That's why I haven't been around. My husband Guillermo and I are separated… and things haven't been right at home."

She reached for a tissue and handed it to me. "Thank you for sharing that with me. You didn't have to—but I'm glad you did."

Then she leaned in, her voice soft but hopeful. "We actually have a few scholarships left. If you're ready, I'd love to help you get back into the program."

I was stunned. Overwhelmed. Grateful. I could barely get the words out, but I nodded through the tears.

"Thank you, thank you," I whispered. "You have no idea what this means to me."

I practically ran to my car in excitement. I couldn't wait to get home and tell *mi tía* about the scholarship. For the first time in a long while, I felt like I was making progress. A part of me wished Guillermo were there to celebrate the good news with me. He had always been supportive of my education.

The plan, or rather our plan, had been for me to earn my nursing license, and then he'd take classes to work toward his engineering certification. But Guillermo was more focused on making money today rather than later.

It still stung, knowing he wasn't here to see it through with me.

****

It had been nearly a month since I last heard from him, and I was starting to worry. No matter what had happened between us, I was still his wife, and he was still their father.

Alberto and Isabelle invited the kids and me over for dinner. While the children played in the backyard, Alberto pulled me aside.

"How are things with you and Guillermo?" he asked gently.

"He hasn't seen the kids in weeks. I know he's upset, but he doesn't have to take it out on them. They didn't ask for any of this." I looked down, unsure of what more to say.

"When I bring you up, he changes the subject. But he did promise he'd reach out soon. He's just…not himself right now."

I swallowed hard, the words hitting me like a punch to the chest. Alberto could've kept that to himself. I wasn't prepared to hear it, but it was good to hear the truth. I nodded slowly, trying to keep my face from giving too much away.

So no clear answer. No visit on the horizon. Just more silence. I was embarrassed—for him, and mostly, disappointed.

"Thank you for telling me," I said quietly.

****

Blue and white balloons and streamers were strung everywhere, draping from doorways and twisting along the banister. The scent of grilled chicken, hot dogs, hamburgers, and sweet plantains floated through the air, carried by bursts of laughter from the backyard. Kids ran through the house, chasing each other with party hats tilted on their heads, squealing with excitement.

At the center of the dining table sat a massive cake, covered in blue and white frosting, with Antonio written across the top in bold, looping letters. Candles surrounded the edge, waiting to be lit.

The mood was festive, but it didn't go unnoticed among the parents, family, and friends that there was one person missing. Guillermo was nowhere in sight.

Still, I smiled and carried on as if it didn't matter. I kept the music playing and laughed when I was supposed to because today was for Antonio.

Just as we gathered around the table, there was a knock at the door. The knock came again and louder this time. The kids paused, mid-chant, their little hands already reaching for the cake.

I wiped my hands on a napkin and walked to the front door, my heart thudding in a rhythm I tried to ignore.

When I opened it, there he was.

Guillermo stood on the porch, holding a gift bag in one hand and a folded card in the other. He looked like he had been debating whether to knock at all. We stood awkwardly at the doorway staring at each other for what seemed like forever.

"Can I come in?" he asked quietly.

For a second, I said nothing. Not because I didn't know what to say, but because there were too many things I wanted to get off my chest that didn't belong at a child's birthday party.

"You're late," I said simply, stepping aside.

He nodded and walked in, eyes scanning the room before landing on Antonio, who stood at the table with wide, stunned eyes.

"Papi!" Antonio yelled, breaking into a run and throwing his arms around his father. Guillermo crouched down, burying his face in his son's shoulder. Antonio and Karime started crying inconsolably. The room was quiet for a moment. Even the music faded into the background.

I turned and walked back to the table, lighting the candles, because no matter what was happening between us, this moment was about Antonio, and he deserved his wish.

Guillermo stuck around after everyone left. He played with Carolina until she fell asleep on his shoulder, and he stayed mainly in the kids' room, while I finished cleaning up. Later, when the kids were in bed asleep, he came into the kitchen and handed me some money.

"I'm sorry, Rosita. I never meant to hurt you. You deserve better," he said quietly.

I didn't respond right away. I just stared at the stack of paper plates in my hand, my back still half-turned to him. There had been too many apologies. Too many broken promises. And yet, a small part of me still wanted to believe he meant it this time.

"Why now?" I asked softly, tossing the used paper plates into the trash. "Why today?"

He leaned against the counter, shoulders slumped. "Because I couldn't miss my son's birthday. Not for anything in the world."

I looked at him, then really looked at him. I missed him so much it hurt, and I had to turn away before he saw it on my face.

"It's getting late." As I walked him to the door, I said, "If you want to show up, then do it—consistently—not just when it's convenient."

"Understood," he said. "I'll stop by in the morning to take the kids to school."

I nodded and opened the door. Without another word exchanged, I watched him get in his car and leave. Then I went to bed feeling empty inside.

Chapter 9

"Dile Que Por Mi No Tema"

The next morning, Guillermo never showed.

By 7:45 AM, I had packed the lunches, tied Karime's braids with pink ribbons, and buckled Carolina into her car seat while Antonio sulked by the door. He didn't ask where his father was, and neither did Karime. The silence hung heavy, like steam in the bathroom after a hot shower, thick, clinging, and impossible to ignore.

I dropped them off like I always did with a kiss on the forehead and a promise that today would be a good day, even if I wasn't sure I believed it myself.

Then I sat in the car for a moment, staring at the steering wheel, debating whether to go back home or do the one thing I knew I had to: go to the school.

I hadn't walked through those glass doors in months. The last time I did, I was a different woman, tired, but hopeful. Now I felt stripped down, like I'd been rebuilt with different parts. Stronger ones, maybe.

The woman at the front desk smiled and waved me toward Ms. Roth's office before I even said a word. "She's expecting you," she said with a wink.

I knocked twice before pushing the door open. Ms. Roth stood and opened her arms. "You ready to come home?"

And just like that, the tears welled up again, only this time, they were filled with hope. I was finally ready to begin this class, one step closer to the nursing program I had dreamed about. My English was getting better, slowly but surely. I was speaking more confidently with my children's teachers, at the grocery store, even when handling bills. Little by little, I was finding my voice in this new world.

Ms. Roth handed me a packet of papers and motioned for me to sit. "We kept your spot open," she said gently. "We knew you'd be back."

I took the seat, still clutching my bag, unsure if I was more nervous or relieved. The classroom buzzed just beyond the door with murmurs, footsteps, and the rustle of notebooks. Life was still happening, and somehow, I was rejoining it.

"I know it hasn't been easy," Ms. Roth continued, "but you're here. That matters."

I nodded, blinking back the tears that threatened to fall again. "Thank you for not giving up on me."

"We don't give up on women like you," she said. "You're the heartbeat of this place."

And for the first time in a long while, I believed her. I stood up, tucked the papers under my arm, and walked out of the office with a steadier stride. This wasn't just about going back to school. It was about reclaiming the parts of myself I thought I'd lost: ambition, dignity, and hope.

I still didn't know where Guillermo was, but for once, I wasn't waiting on him to show up.

I was showing up for myself.

****

The excitement from class had spilled over, and I was eager to dive into my homework. I had a few hours before picking up Antonio and Karime, and after putting Carolina down for her nap, I settled in to start my assignment.

Then came a knock at the door.

I looked out and saw Guillermo. I opened it slowly.

"What happened this morning?" I asked as he stepped inside.

"I had a car accident," he said.

"Oh my God, are you okay?"

"I'm fine. The insurance said they'll take care of it."

"Why didn't you call?"

"Check your messages," he replied. "*¿Y dónde está Carolina?*"

"I put her down for a nap."

He glanced around, then looked at me more seriously.

I folded my arms. "Guillermo… The kids are disappointed in you."

"I'm not here to argue," he said quickly. "I just wanted to let you know I'll pick the kids up from school today."

He paused, his voice softening. "Rosita, I miss you. I'm trying to do better. You just have to believe me. I love you, and I love our children. I miss my family."

I stared at him, unsure of what to say. Part of me wanted to believe him and wanted to hold on to the version of Guillermo I used to know. The one who made the kids laugh until their bellies hurt, who danced with me in the kitchen while dinner simmered on the stove. But that version had been missing for a long time.

"*No vale la pena*," I said.

He nodded slowly, looking down at the floor.

"I'm not saying this to hurt you," I continued, "but I have to protect our children from inconsistency. They need stability. I need stability."

"I understand," he said. "I just want a chance to make things right."

"You don't get to fix everything in a day, Guillermo. Picking them up from school isn't a magic solution. It's consistency. It's presence. It's showing up again and again."

He took a step back, nodding. "Okay. I'll see you later, then."

I didn't stop him as he turned to leave. I just watched the door close behind him, then walked quietly to the bedroom to check on Carolina.

I stood in the doorway for a moment, watching Carolina sleep, her soft curls splayed across the pillow. She was still asleep, her tiny chest rising and falling with the rhythm of peace I was fighting so hard to preserve. The innocence in her face reminded me of what all of this was for—why I kept going, even when it felt like I was piecing my life together with tape and prayer.

I walked back to the kitchen, poured myself a glass of juice, and sat at the table with my notebook. The pages were still blank, the assignment untouched. I stared at the first question, trying to will myself back into focus. But my mind kept drifting to Guillermo's words, his face, the weight behind his voice.

Did he mean it this time? How many times had I asked myself that same question?

I took a deep breath, picked up my pen, and started writing not for the assignment, but for me. A letter, a release, maybe even a goodbye. Something about seeing the truth on paper made it easier to face. Because I knew one thing for sure: I couldn't go backward. Not now. Not when I was just starting to remember who I was before everything fell apart—and who I might still become.

The sound of Carolina crying broke the silence. I wiped a tear from my cheek and stood up, already switching gears from student to mother. There would be time to finish the assignment later.

While I was changing Carolina's diaper, the school called. No one had come to pick up Antonio and Karime.

¡Coño, Guillermo! Your word means nothing anymore.

By the time I picked up Antonio and Karime from school, the sun had dipped low in the sky, casting long shadows across the pavement. They rushed toward me with their usual energy, Karime waving a crumpled drawing in the air, and Antonio dragging his backpack by one strap.

"Guess what we did today!" Karime exclaimed, practically bouncing into the car.

Antonio climbed in quietly, but gave me a knowing glance, one I couldn't quite read. Not yet.

I smiled and listened as Karime rattled off the details of her day in her small voice. It always came heavy with memories that refused to stay tucked away. But Karime, in her bright, effortless way, knew just how to break through it.

"Mami, we're celebrating Hispanic Heritage Month at school," she said, her tone rising with excitement.

"That's wonderful, *mi amor*," I replied and gave her my full attention.

"Please, can we not bring guava and crackers this time?"

I raised an eyebrow, surprised. "Why not? I thought the kids loved it."

"They do," she said, drawing out the words with a dramatic sigh, "but surely you can think of something else. Something better. Something that makes them go wow."

I laughed softly. "Wow, huh? Since when did guava and crackers stop being enough?"

She shrugged, twirling a strand of hair around her finger. "I just want them to know there's more to us than snacks, Mami. You always say food tells a story, so let's tell a better one."

Her words caught me off guard, not because they weren't true, but because they came from such a small body with such a big spirit. Guillermo would've loved this moment. He would've called her a firecracker, pulled her close, and promised to make some croquetas from scratch just to see her beam.

I blinked back the sting in my eyes and smiled instead. "Alright, storyteller. We'll come up with something that makes them say wow."

Thank goodness I'd told the kids I'd be there, just in case Guillermo disappeared again. Maybe that was growth, or maybe it was the kind of tiredness that seeps into your psyche. Only God knows.

When we got home, I reheated leftover picadillo with white rice and black beans, while they started their homework at the table. Carolina toddled around the living room, dragging her stuffed bunny by the ear, laughing at nothing in particular.

For a moment, life felt normal. Simple. Manageable.

After dinner, when the kids were finally tucked in and the house had gone quiet, I returned to the notebook I had started earlier that day. The half-written letter still sat there, raw and unfiltered. But now, I flipped to a fresh page and began again.

This time, it was for my future.

My story.

My terms.

La verdad.

For the first time in a long time, I wasn't just surviving, I was rebuilding.

Word by word.

And this time, I wasn't waiting for anyone to save me.

Chapter 10

"¿Por Qué Será?"

Isabelle and Alberto invited me and the kids over for dinner. As soon as we arrived, Alberto gently directed the children to go play in their rooms. The moment the door clicked shut behind them, I sensed something was coming, something serious about Guillermo.

Alberto didn't waste time. "I had to let him go," he said, his voice low but steady. "I think Guillermo is using. I didn't want to believe it at first. I gave him chance after chance, but the signs were all there: missed shifts, money missing and slurred words."

Isabelle looked down, twisting her wedding ring in slow, anxious circles. My heart sank. Heat rushed to my face as a mix of dread and disbelief washed over me.

"I'm sorry, Rosita," Alberto said. "At first, I thought it was just the drinking. But now…I'm not so sure. We believe it could be crack cocaine. Some of the construction crew saw him hanging out in an area where it's sold."

"He didn't use drugs in Cuba," I said.

"This drug is so powerful that you can become addicted to it on the first try," Alberto explained.

I sat there in stunned silence, the sound of the children laughing faintly in the background, innocent and unaware, cutting through the heavy moment like a cruel reminder of what was at stake.

"Have you noticed anything?" Isabelle asked gently.

I nodded, my voice barely above a whisper. "He'd been distant for a while and completely absent for all those weeks. He doesn't show up when he says he will for the kids. I thought it was the stress…and maybe someone else was involved, like another woman."

Alberto leaned forward, his tone urgent but kind. "We care about you. About the kids. That's why we're telling you. He needs help, but he won't get there unless he sees how far he's fallen."

I swallowed hard, a knot tightening deep in my stomach. I had been trying to hold everything together, but at that moment, I knew I couldn't ignore it any longer.

"I've been told he's living in a shelter," Alberto said.

"How can I get him help if I don't know how to reach him?" I asked, my voice cracking.

Isabelle reached across the table and took my hand. "You can't force him, Rosita. He has to want the help. But you can set boundaries for yourself, and for the kids."

I looked down at my lap, holding back my tears. "I don't even know who he is anymore. I love him so much that I'm trying to fix him, while he's breaking me apart.

Alberto nodded. "There are programs. Outreach workers who visit shelters, clinics that offer counseling and detox. If he's ready, he'll find his way there. But you can't sacrifice yourself trying to save him."

"I know, but he's my husband, and if he is sick and has an addiction…

"You know who you are," Isabelle said gently. "And you've got those babies depending on you. That's where your energy has to go now."

I nodded slowly. It wasn't the advice I wanted, but it was the one I needed.

Later that night, after I tucked the kids into bed and I sat alone in the living room, the tears came. Not just for Guillermo, but for the life I thought we were building. If I had known our relationship would unravel like this, that he would lose himself to addiction, I might have stayed in Cuba. By no means was life there perfect, but at least it was something familiar. Besides, I would rather know the crazy I knew before than this crazy that I didn't know.

I cried for the man I thought I knew and for the version of myself that still held onto the hope he'd walk through the door and make it right.

But beneath the grief was a deeper, sharper pain. I didn't know what the road ahead would bring, but I knew one thing for certain: something had to give.

****

I went home feeling numb, and the conversation with Alberto and Isabelle ran on repeat in my head. I didn't know what to do. As a wife, I felt compelled to help Guillermo, so while the kids stayed a few days with Alberto and Isabelle, I drove around the city looking for him. I was so determined to find him, it never occurred to me that I might not.

It was exhausting checking the usual corners, asking questions at bodegas, scanning shelters and side streets, following rumors like I was the KGB. Every time I thought I was getting close, he slipped through my fingers like smoke. Still, I couldn't bring myself to stop. Something in me needed to see him, to look him in the eyes and ask the questions my heart wasn't ready to answer.

By the third day, my hope was wearing thin. My gas tank hovered near empty, and so did my spirit. I parked outside the old church on Fourth and just sat there, hands on the wheel, staring blankly through the windshield. The city moved around me, horns blaring, people rushing past, but I felt completely still, like I was floating outside of time.

Then I saw him. Guillermo shuffled past the corner store, head down, his coat hanging off him like it didn't belong to him anymore. His walk was slower, with his shoulders hunched. My heart pounded. I didn't call out. I didn't honk. I just stepped out of the car and started walking toward him, each step heavy with everything unsaid.

"Guillermo," I called softly.

He froze. His back straightened slightly, but he didn't turn around right away. When he finally did, his eyes were tired. Not just from lack of sleep or hunger, but from shame. From running. From the things he couldn't fix.

"Rosita," he whispered, like saying my name hurt. "You shouldn't be here."

"I didn't come to fight," I said. "I came to find you."

He looked away, wiping his nose with the sleeve of his coat. "Why?"

Because I still loved him. I remembered the man who held my hand on the boat from Cuba and promised we'd build a life. Because no matter how far he had fallen, he was still the father of my children. But I couldn't say all of that. Not yet.

"Because you're my husband," I said instead.

He nodded, barely. "I'm not the man you married."

"No," I said. "And I'm not the same woman either."

The tension between us slowly began to fade, but it wasn't empty. Instead, it was full of memories, pain, and the faintest trace of hope. I reached into my coat pocket and pulled out a sandwich I had made that morning. I held it out to him.

"Come home," I said. "Or at least…come inside. We can sit. Talk. Eat."

He hesitated, then took the sandwich. And for the first time in months, I saw something different in his eyes. Not joy. Not peace.

He walked into the house and looked around, his eyes scanning each corner like he didn't recognize the place anymore. He looked nervous.

"Where are the kids?" he asked.

"They're at a friend's house and Carolina's with them too," I replied. I didn't want him to know the kids were with Alberto and Isabelle.

He nodded, visibly relieved that the children weren't around.

The smell hit me before he even sat down. He reeked of the street, sweat, smoke, and something heavier. I quietly ran him a bath and started cooking his favorite meal.

"There are clean clothes in the hallway closet. They might be a little loose. You've lost weight. I handed him a towel. He gave me a faint smile, almost embarrassed, and disappeared down the hallway.

When he returned, he looked cleaner, yet still worn. Dressed in sweatpants and an old T-shirt, he was a shadow of the man I married, yet still my husband, still Guillermo. His body was frail, his face gaunt, his lips dry and cracked. I could hardly believe what this drug had done to him.

He sat at the table and devoured his food like he hadn't eaten in days. I watched him, my heart breaking a little with every bite he took.

"Guillermo," I said gently, "there's more food. You don't have to rush."

He set his fork down for a moment, as if realizing for the first time that he was safe at least for now. His hands trembled slightly as he reached for his glass of water.

"I didn't know if you'd ever allow me back in," he said, his voice low.

He stared at his plate, ashamed, and for a long while, neither of us spoke. The only sounds were the ticking of the kitchen clock and the faint hum of the refrigerator.

Finally, he whispered, "I'm sorry, Rosita. I never meant for things to get this bad."

I swallowed the lump in my throat. "I know," I said. "But it did, and now we have to figure out what comes next."

He looked up at me then, his eyes filled with a mixture of fear and something else, something fragile. Hope, maybe.

"We," he repeated, almost to himself. Like he wasn't sure he deserved the word.

"Yes," I said firmly, "we."

I cleared the table while he sat there, quiet, like he was afraid to move and break the moment.

I stood by the sink, hands resting on the counter, staring out the window into the night. Part of me wanted to believe that feeding him, bathing him, offering kindness would be enough. But I knew better. Love alone couldn't fix this.

"You can sleep on the couch," I offered.

He looked at me, surprised. Not hurt. Just surprised. "I want you to rest," I added. "We'll talk more tomorrow."

He nodded and sat back down. "Rosita… Do you really think we can come back from this?"

I walked toward the hallway, pausing at the door. "I don't know," I said honestly. "But I know I'm willing to try. One day at a time."

He looked down at his hands, then back up at me. "So am I."

And for the first time in a long time, we let our inner thoughts hold us not in tension, but in stillness. Two people trying. Two people starting all over again.

****

The next morning, I woke up and Guillermo was gone, and so was all of the money in my purse. My heart sank, but I wasn't surprised. That would become the pattern: brief moments of hope, followed by disappointment.

For years, we were caught in that cycle. Guillermo slipped in and out of the streets, and sometimes, on a good day, I managed to encourage him to enter into one of those rundown city rehabs. Crack was so new then that most counselors had no idea how to fight it, and the few programs that showed promise were cut before they could even work. He would come back with apologies dressed up as promises he could never keep. Each time he swore it was the last, and each time, against my better judgment, I wanted to believe him. Sometimes, I did.

It wasn't until a run-in with the law, a night that could have ended so much worse, that something inside him finally shifted. Guillermo spent sixty days behind bars with one year of probation. It could have been longer if not for the money I borrowed from Yasmine to pay for a good lawyer.

Maybe it was fear. Maybe it was grace. But from that point on, he started to change. He still drank beer now and then, but the drugs, the women, the drama, he left behind.

Slowly, painstakingly, he began to piece himself back together. He found steady work as a custodian. A friend of a friend recommended him to the local high school, where he was revered by both students and staff. Students often sought his advice, and when someone acted out, it was Guillermo they called to set things straight.

On days when a student didn't have lunch, he'd reach into his pocket and make sure they were taken care of. But with his own children, the path was rougher. Years of absence and broken promises had left scars that didn't fade easily.

They didn't trust him, not right away. Carolina barely spoke to him. She was too young to remember Guillermo who made everyone laugh. She only knew him as the father who struggled with drugs. Antonio kept his distance, watching with cautious eyes, but Guillermo didn't push. He knew he was on the verge of losing his family for good.

We had grown accustomed to his absence. The excuses had run out, so he made sure to show up at every parent-teacher conference, every school event, every family dinner. He was a father again, and the man I always knew he could be.

It took time, but eventually, the kids began to let him in again. Carolina would ask him for help with her school projects. Antonio started spending more time with him, surfing baseball games on the couch. Little by little, the cracks started to close.

Our oldest, Karime, never cared about his past. She loved him fiercely and without conditions. Guillermo affectionately called her his soldier. Out of our three children, she was the truest daddy's girl and, in personality, the one most like me.

During his battles with addiction, Karime would often ask if she could go out and find him. It broke my heart every time she asked. I would gently remind her that her daddy loved her and would be back soon.

When it came to discipline, she had him completely wrapped around her finger, getting away with more than the others ever could. She was his favorite, and all the kids knew it.

As for Guillermo and me, we found our way back to each other, too. It took a long time, and not without struggle. He slept on the couch many nights. There were still days when old wounds ached and tempers flared. But there was laughter again, forgiveness, and something tender, something hard won and precious. It felt a lot like peace.

****

For years, I avoided asking who had first led him to crack, afraid the truth would reopen wounds I wasn't ready to face. I didn't ask, and he didn't offer. Then one afternoon, Guillermo seemed unsettled, over un cafecito and the newspaper spread across the table, he said her name.

"*¿Cómo?*"

"Sandra."

"*¿Sandra? ¡Coño*, Guillermo! After all these years, why the hell are you bringing her up?"

"She's the one who introduced me to crack," he muttered, dropping his head.

"*¿Y nosotros, ah?* Wasn't this *hogar*, this *vida*, enough for you?"

"*Claro que sí*, Rosita. *Pero*, I tried it once or twice…and yeah, I wanted *más*. I couldn't stop. It was that *fuerte*."

"*¿Y ahora por qué?* You slipping *otra vez? Han pasado años*, Guillermo. You've been holding it down."

"*No, mi vida. Para nada.* I just need you to know I'd never choose *drogas ni otra mujer* over you and the kids. Biggest mistake *de mi vida*."

"We forgave you, Guillermo. *Eso se quedó atrás*. We're blessed. *Tenemos lo nuestro.* Life is good…*aunque el billete, bueno, siempre podría ser mejor*."

He looked me in the eyes and reached across the table. The steam from the *cafecito* curled between us, sweet and bitter all at once. I froze. Her name had already cut through me like a bullet, and now his words pressed even deeper. Rage rose in my chest. I wanted to grab a *chancleta* and hurl it at him, to smash the years of anger I had swallowed. But beneath the fury was a quieter ache—a part of me that believed him, that love and prayers had saved us.

My fingers trembled around the warm porcelain cup. The only sounds were the ticking clock and the faint hum of traffic outside. He said nothing more, and I understood. He had carried that ghost so long it had nearly broken us both. We never spoke of it again.

Chapter 11

"Te Busco"

After all the years I let slip by, I finally enrolled in the last class I needed to sit before taking the NCLEX nursing board exam. I had worked as a waitress at a local diner for quite a number of years. The tips were nice, but they were only a small part of what our family needed to make ends meet. Guillermo's salary made it a bit better; although he didn't earn much, it was steady, and his job with the school provided health insurance.

Thanks to *tia*, Yasmine, and Pedro, who had been a tremendous support over the years, we were able to hold everything together. I knew this wasn't by accident that we were getting the support we needed. I knew so many people came to this country and had no support. Alberto and Isabelle never gave up on us, and no deed went unnoticed. I didn't take for granted the blessings that had come our way, and I prayed that one day I'd be able to pay it forward.

But at that moment in our lives, it was time to finish what I had started. More than anything, I wanted to show my children how important it is to have an education.

The thought of walking into a classroom again, surrounded by students young enough to be my children, made my stomach twist with doubt. Still, I was tired of putting my dreams on hold. I had survived so much already—surely, I could survive a few late nights and a handful of exams. As I filled out the registration form, my hands trembled, but my heart felt steady. This was my time.

My shadow, Carolina, was growing up before my eyes. Karime was preparing to enter high school, with Antonio not far behind her. My oldest, Karime, was gifted, but the neighborhood schools were not equipped to nurture her talent. Yasmine suggested she come live with them so she could attend school in their neighborhood in Miami. In America, the quality of a child's education too often depends on their zip code.

Our neighborhood had changed over the years, and after the white families moved out, the schools began to deteriorate, and the school-to-prison pipeline became painfully evident. Resources dried up, good teachers moved away, and what was left behind was a system barely holding itself together. I wanted more for Karime—for all of my children. I wanted her to know that her dreams didn't have to shrink to fit the limits of our zip code. So, when Yasmine offered to take Karime in so she could attend a better school in Miami, I said yes, even though it broke my heart a little that my child would be far away from me. I knew she would be in good hands. She would be with family.

Over the following school year, the house felt emptier without Karime's laughter through the rooms, but every phone call, every visit reminded me that we had made the right decision. She was thriving. She was dreaming bigger. And in her voice, I heard the future calling for all of us.

It wasn't just Karime's journey that mattered; it was mine too. I realized that the best way to teach my children about perseverance, about faith, about chasing something better, was to live by that rule.

So, on the first day of my new class, as I stood outside the building holding on to my books and peering through the glass window at the door, fear tried to take over me. Still, it didn't stand a chance against the hope and determination that had carried me this far. I wasn't just going back to school—I was stepping into the life I had always wanted for me, and for them.

***

I had just earned an A on my first exam in Microbiology, one of the toughest classes in the nursing program. Not many students passed that first test, and I was proud. It felt like proof that I belonged, that all the sacrifices were starting to mean something.

There were nights I stayed up long after everyone had gone to bed, hunched over my textbooks, fighting off the doubts that crept in when I was alone.

Guillermo would sometimes wake up and find me still at the kitchen table. "Come to bed, *mi amor*," he'd whisper. "Tomorrow is a new day."

He knew how much this course meant to me, how badly I wanted to finish what I started, not just for myself, but for all of us.

My class met twice a week, and on those days, Guillermo would take care of dinner, either cooking or ordering Chinese takeout. He would even have my bathwater ready for me. Afterward, we would all sit together in the living room and watch our favorite show, *The Cosby Show*, while we ate dinner. It was the first time I had seen a family on television that looked like mine and shared the same values.

"*Me encanta* the beautiful woman who played the wife, Claire Huxtable." I admired her character so much. I tried to emulate her in the way she dressed, the way she spoke, the graceful way she carried herself. I even had Carmen cut my hair like hers, with my hair layered going back. She was an inspiration, a reminder that I could succeed at anything, at being a mother, a wife, and so much more. And Cliff Huxtable? He reminded me so much of my

Guillermo, with his humor and wit. In their children, I even saw bits and pieces of my own children, especially their laughter and mischief.

****

While I was winning in class, my home life began to shift, and Guillermo had to pick up the pieces where I was neglecting. One afternoon, while I was at school, Antonio had been caught stealing from a corner store with a group of boys from his school. A fight ensued. Guillermo rushed to the station, spoke with the police, and handled everything without telling me. He made the decision to shield me from the news, worried that the stress might pull my focus from my classes. It wasn't until weeks later that I found out.

I came home early one afternoon and found Guillermo in the kitchen, chopping vegetables for dinner. I placed my bag down harder than I meant to, even though I was upset.

"Why didn't you tell me about Antonio?" I demanded, my voice sharper than I intended.

Guillermo froze, the knife still in his hand. He turned slowly, meeting my eyes. "You had enough on your plate, Rosita," he said gently. "I didn't want to burden you."

"Burden me?" I shook my head, the hurt rising in my throat. "He's our son, Guillermo. I deserved to know."

He set the knife down carefully and wiped his hands on a dish towel. "I know," he said, stepping closer. "I was wrong to keep it from you. But I was scared. Scared it would distract you…scared it might pull you away from what we're fighting for."

I crossed my arms, trying to hold myself together. "I'm his mother. I need to be there, good or bad. We're supposed to do this together. Nothing comes before our children.

Guillermo nodded. His voice broke just a little when he said, "I was trying to protect you. Maybe I didn't do it the right way, but everything I do, everything is for you and these kids."

"Protect me?" My hands balled into fists at my sides. "I needed to know."

The anger simmered in my chest, but it was tangled now with something else: love, and sorrow, and the impossible choices we were both making. I stared at him, the anger diminishing under the weight of his confession.

He let out a slow breath, the lines on his face deeper than usual. "When I was Antonio's age," he said, his voice low, "I got caught stealing too. The only difference was, nobody gave me a second chance. No talks, no warnings. I wasn't going to allow that for my son.

"I saw Antonio in that police station," Guillermo continued, "scared, ashamed. I remembered how it felt. And all I could think was not him. Not my boy. Not if I could help it." His voice cracked then, just slightly. "I thought…if I could handle it, you could keep your eyes on the prize. Finish school. Get us somewhere better."

I swallowed hard, feeling my chest tighten.

"I'm sorry, Rosita," he said, stepping closer. "Maybe I went about it the wrong way, but every decision I made, I made for you. For us."

The kitchen seemed to shrink around us, heavy with unsaid things. I wanted to hold on to my anger, but all I felt was sadness for him, for Antonio, for all the ways life had demanded we be strong.

Later that night, after the kids were in bed, Guillermo drew a bath for me. He didn't say much. He just placed a warm towel nearby, lit a small fragrant candle, and kissed my forehead before leaving me to myself. I sank into the water, letting the tears I had been holding finally fall.

It wasn't the end of our challenges, but it was a turning point. We all grew from it, a reminder that even in a family built on dreams, trust, and love, mistakes could hurt, but they could also heal.

Antonio, for his part, seemed to learn from the scare. He started waking up earlier, offering to help around the house, even asking to tag along with Guillermo on weekends to learn responsibility. He didn't talk much about what happened, but the shame and determination were clear in his eyes. From this incident, Antonio and Guillermo grew closer as father and son.

I was more determined than ever to finish school, but it hurt to make such difficult decisions for my children. Guillermo and I gave Antonio two choices: he could either go live with Yasmine or transfer to a different school district. No way was he going to stay in that school or continue to hang out with those kids. When he chose to stay, I felt a small sense of relief, but I knew the road ahead wouldn't be easy. Guillermo and I were frightened of those societal traps that could be revoked at a moment's notice. We refused to allow our only son to go down that pathway.

Through a lottery system, we were able to enroll both Antonio and Carolina in a busing program, sending them to schools in another county, several miles away from home, in communities where fewer students looked like them. At first, they felt like outsiders, as if they were just occupying seats rather than truly belonging. Carolina, however, adjusted quickly. She made new friends with ease, and her teachers adored her. I suppose Carolina fit right in because of her lighter skin. Carolina and Karime took after my grandmother, who was a *mulata* with long, wavy hair.

Antonio, on the other hand, whose skin color was more bronze, a shade darker than mine and lighter than Guillermo's, with coily textured hair, struggled at first. I kept getting calls daily from the school. It took time, but eventually he found his footing, and once he started playing Lacrosse and basketball with immense talent, everything began to change. Antonio knew athletics could be his ticket to college, so he doubled down, becoming even more committed to improving his game. Playing sports was how

Antonio learned their respect, not because he made the honor roll throughout his four years in high school,

Then the house party invitations started rolling in, and I got nervous. It didn't take long for me to recognize that Black boys in America walk through life with a target on their backs. I knew I couldn't shield him from everything, but I was determined to protect mine as much as I could.

"He's not a little boy anymore," Guillermo would remind me. "We have to trust that we raised him right." And I did. Still, trusting him wasn't the hard part—it was trusting the world around him.

For the first time, our kids began to notice that our lives were vastly different from their classmates. They were mostly white, affluent and surrounded by resources and privilege that often opened doors before they even had to knock.

One day, Antonio said, "Some of my friends have everything, big houses, new bikes, all that. But they don't have what I have. They don't have parents who love them like you and Papi love me."

I held onto those words for dear life. During my alone time, when I questioned whether all of the sacrifices were worth it, I thought of Antonio's voice and remembered, we were giving them something more valuable than money; we were giving them a foundation built on love, trust and sacrifice.

****

Even in those darkest moments when doubt crept in, Guillermo had a way of grounding me, reminding me that love, in all its forms, still lived between us.

I was in a deep sleep when I felt Guillermo press his body gently against mine. He lifted my nightgown with the tenderness that only he could do, and whispered, "I need you." My eyes stayed closed, but I felt everything: his warmth, his longing, the subtle way he reminded me I was still his *negrita bella*. Every time he touched me like that, it wasn't just desire. It was love, steady and deep, pulling me closer even in sleep.

We made love more than once that night, as if trying to reclaim something that hadn't even been lost, just tucked beneath the weight of everyday life. It hadn't been long since the last time, barely a day, but somehow, it still felt like we had been starving. Maybe it was the stress, or the silence we sometimes kept between us. In those moments, none of that mattered.

Afterward, we lay tangled in the sheets, our breathing soft, the room still. I stared at the ceiling, my fingers caressing his chest. I thought about how much we'd both sacrificed to hold our family together and how intimacy became our way of remembering who we were before the struggles and long nights. Before life tried to harden us.

Guillermo pulled me closer and kissed me. "You're my everything," he whispered. And in that moment, I believed it not just because of the words, but because of how he showed me, over and over again.

As I walked out of the room, Guillermo playfully slapped my butt, and in return, I stuck my tongue out at him and jokingly ran out of the room to make breakfast before heading out to the airport.

****

When we arrived at the airline's gate, we saw Karime from a distance running toward us. I couldn't believe my firstborn had grown up. She had only been away for a few months, but everything about her had changed, even her hair, which had grown past her shoulders. She was wearing a little makeup, and her mannerisms were different and more refined. The way she spoke was proper, and no Cuban accent could be detected. It felt almost rehearsed, like she had learned to carry herself in a new world we didn't fully know.

I reached out to hug her, and for a moment, I held on a little longer than usual, trying to feel if the girl I gave birth to and raised was still in there. Her scent, her smile, they were familiar, but she was becoming her own person. And that, more than anything, made my heart swell with pride.

Over dinner, Karime casually mentioned that Yasmine and Pedro had a nanny who cooked their meals and made sure they bathed and ate on time. I smiled and listened, stirring the pot on the stove, trying not to let the comment stay too long in my mind.

I knew my cousin's schedule was relentless. She was now the chief surgeon at the University of Miami Hospital, a title she had worked hard to earn. She didn't have the time to do all the little things I did for my kids: packing lunches with handwritten notes, braiding hair before school, whispering prayers over sleeping foreheads.

Sometimes, I wondered if my children noticed the difference. If deep down, they desired a life of luxury that comes with help and more ease. But then Karime would hug me out of nowhere, or Carolina would bring home a drawing that looked suspiciously like me, crown and all, and I'd be reminded: I was enough. Antonio said one day that he knew me and Guillermo were in the stands, and that's what made him go for the winning shot.

I was grateful for everything my cousin had done for our family—her generosity, her strength, her example. I was also proud of the life that I was building, one that didn't mirror hers at all.

****

"I have a boyfriend," Karime blurted out as we sat waiting for the next nail technician.

I looked over at her, startled, but not entirely surprised. She was seventeen, after all. Still, my mind immediately went to Guillermo. I wasn't sure he was ready to hear about this just yet.

"So," I said, keeping my tone even, "tell me about him."

"His name is Jeremy, and his parents are from the Bahamas," she said, a soft smile spreading across her face. "Mom, he's really smart. He's on the Dean's List, and he wants to be a cardiologist. He's applying to Harvard, Princeton, Brown, and the University of Miami."

"Impressive," I said, nodding slowly. "Does he treat you well?"

"Yes, Mami. He's really sweet."

"Have you introduced him to Tía Yasmine and Tío Pedro?"

"Yeah, Tía Yasmine liked him. She said he seemed like a nice guy."

"And your Uncle Pedro?"

Karime hesitated. "I think so. He didn't say much, but he was kind."

In my head, I wasn't surprised. Pedro had always been guarded. Something I couldn't explain.

"I know you introduced him to *mi tia*, right?"

Karime laughed. "Tia said I did good and winked at me when he wasn't looking."

I studied her face for a moment, the way her eyes lit up when she talked about him, the calm certainty in her voice. Part of me wanted to protect her from everything: heartbreak, disappointment, the weight of first love. Another part, the wiser part, knew this was hers to experience.

"Well," I said finally, squeezing her hand, "just make sure he keeps treating you that way. You're worth that and more."

She smiled again, and in that moment, I saw both the little girl she used to be and the young woman she was becoming. Just then, the nail technician signaled for us to come over, pulling my attention back to the present and to the chipped nail that had brought us here in the first place.

As we settled into our chairs, Karime looked over at me. "Are you okay, Mami?"

I nodded, staring at the bright bottles of polish lined up like candy on the shelf. "Just thinking," I said.

"About Jeremy?"

I laughed softly. "A little. But mostly about how fast time goes. One minute I'm tying your shoes, and the next you're telling me about your college-bound boyfriend."

She reached for my hand and gave it a squeeze. "I'm still your little girl. I promise."

And even though I knew that promise would one day fade, I held onto it for now.

"Mami, may I ask you a question?"

"*Dime, mi vida.*"

"How did you and Papi meet?"

I chuckled at her curiosity. "Well, according to Papi, he loved me long before I even knew he existed. He swears it was my glasses—said they must not have been working right."

She smiled. "He told me the same thing when he shared your story."

I looked at her, studying the way her face lit up when we talked about love. There was something tender in her expression, like she was collecting pieces of a puzzle about who she was and where she came from.

"Back then," I continued, "I was so focused on school and trying to stay out of trouble that I didn't even notice he was watching me. But your papi was patient. Kind of relentless, actually. He found little ways to show up, to be near me."

I looked away and shook my head, blushing like a schoolgirl guarding a precious secret. My heart fluttered with excitement, my palms suddenly sweaty just like the day Guillermo and I first met in the schoolyard. As I continued to speak, I searched for the right words, not wanting to leave out a single part of our love story.

"We went to school together. Guillermo was popular, especially with the girls. He had this natural charm and confidence that drew people to him. I was the opposite. Quiet, awkward, reserved, lost in my books. Studying was my escape, the only thing that gave me hope in a place where so many dreams felt impossible.

"One afternoon, he came up to me and asked if he could walk me home. I didn't know what to say; I was too shy to turn him away. He was so handsome, but it was something about his presence that made me feel seen like never before.

"That first walk turned into many. Day after day, he waited for me after class, and somehow, he always made me laugh. For a moment, the heaviness of life in Cuba felt lighter. Then my father found out. He didn't like the idea of me walking home with a boy, especially one with a reputation. He warned me there'd be consequences if it continued."

"Why, Mami?"

"He'd heard about Guillermo and the crowd he ran with, always up to no good, as my father used to say. In his eyes, no man was ever worthy of my love. My father was a complicated man, a *comandante* in the military, one of the very reasons my mother left him. They envisioned life so differently.

"Still, I knew he loved me, and I believe he did the best he could under the weight of the circumstances he had faced. My parents separated, and not long after, when I was ten, my mother passed away. From then on, he raised me alone. He was strict and fiercely protective, convinced I was too good for someone like Guillermo. Truth be told, even Guillermo felt the same way at times.

"I tried to avoid Guillermo after that, but he wasn't easily discouraged. The next day, he stood at the school gates, waiting just like always. I whispered, 'You can't walk me home anymore. My father found out.' He looked at me, a little hurt but not surprised. 'Is he mad because of me?' I nodded, "I understand." He stepped aside then and said, 'I'll still wait. Just in case you change your mind.'

"And he did. Every day, he waited with a flower in hand. Some days I'd walk past him without a word. Other days, I'd smile shyly, my heart aching with longing and fear. I didn't know what this was yet, but it was something. Something real.

"Eventually, my father noticed I was coming home miserable and lonelier. One evening, he asked, 'Where's the boy who used to make you smile?' I hesitated, unsure if it was a trap. 'I told him not to walk me home anymore,' I finally replied, and my father sighed. 'You're still young. Just make sure he respects you. That's all I ask.'

"I can still see it like it happened just yesterday. My papi was wearing his olive-green cap and military fatigues, an old long-sleeved button-up shirt with chest pockets, straight-leg trousers, and black combat boots. He sat on a wooden chair on the porch, which creaked as he shifted in his seat, puffing on a cigar nearly as long as two fingers pressed together and sipping his Havana Club. In disbelief, I watched as he exhaled a slow stream of smoke rings into the air.

"The next day, I waited for Guillermo, and when he saw me, his whole face lit up. Before I knew it, he wasn't just part of my world; he was my world. We became inseparable, and a few years later, I became pregnant with you. The rest, as they say, is history."

Karime leaned her head on my shoulder. "That's beautiful, Mami."

Her face glowed with happiness. As I watched my daughter, I wanted her to understand that the love I shared with Guillermo hadn't always been easy. It came with its share of bumps along the way. And while I cherished our journey, I wanted something different for her. I wanted her to enjoy this season of her life, to have fun and date, while focusing on her studies and not get tied down like I did. While I had no regrets, sometimes I felt like I was robbed of my youth. Guillermo and I weren't ready for the responsibility that came with marriage and being parents. We were kids ourselves.

A few minutes after I finished my story, a petite, middle-aged Asian woman interrupted our conversation and motioned for us to take our seats at the pedicure chairs.

"Have you talked to your dad about Jeremy?" I asked.

"No."

"Why not?"

"I just haven't had a chance," she said, avoiding my eyes.

But I knew the truth. She was putting it off. Avoiding the conversation, afraid her dad would have issues with her dating.

Later that evening, I pulled Guillermo aside and made him promise not to bring up anything about a boyfriend, not yet. "She'll tell you when she's ready," I said gently.

He looked at me, his brows slightly raised, but nodded. "Alright. I'll wait."

It wasn't easy for him, letting go of control, staying quiet. But for Karime's sake, he would.

****

We were all watching *The Cosby Show* as we typically did on a Thursday night, when Denise Huxtable appeared on screen, deep in conversation with her boyfriend. Without warning, Carolina blurted out, "Karime has a boyfriend too! His name is Jeremy."

Karime's face flushed with embarrassment. "No, I don't," she snapped, eyes wide with panic.

"Yes, you do," Carolina insisted. "I heard you on the phone with him last night! 'Jeremy'", she mocked.

Before I could step in, Antonio jumped in with a scowl. "Carolina, mind your business. You're just mad because nobody likes you."

"Okay," I said calmly, reaching for the remote and lowering the volume. "That's enough."

Everyone became quiet, lost in their thoughts. Karime stared at her lap, her cheeks still burning. Carolina crossed her arms, clearly unbothered, while Antonio looked proud of himself for jumping to his sister's defense.

Guillermo looked over at me, one eyebrow slightly raised. I shook my head just enough for him to catch the signal—not now.

He took a breath, then turned to Carolina. "We don't put each other on blast like that," he said, his tone firm but even. "Especially not in front of the whole family."

Carolina mumbled a half-hearted apology. "I'm sorry, Karime." Karime still hadn't looked up.

I reached over and touched her hand. "It's alright, *mi amor*. We'll talk later, just you and me."

She nodded, barely. I saw the girl who was still trying to figure out how much of her life she could share with her parents.

Later that evening, I overheard Guillermo and Karime laughing and talking in the living room. Their voices floated down the hallway, light and filled with ease. I paused for a moment, just out of sight, listening.

"So, this Jeremy," Guillermo said, his tone even and curious, "he treats you right?"

"Yes, Papi," Karime replied, a smile in her voice. "He's really sweet. And we're taking it slow. I promise."

There was a short pause before Guillermo responded, "Good. That's all I needed to hear."

I was so proud of Guillermo that he hadn't come down hard on her or grilled her or turned the moment into a lecture. He gave her space to be honest, and she trusted him enough to take it. That's what mattered most.

In that moment, I saw the progress we'd made as parents, learning when to speak, when to listen, and how to build trust without fear. It wasn't always perfect, but tonight, it felt like we got it right this time.

A few weeks later, we saw Karime off at the airport as she headed back to Miami. I already knew I was going to miss her deeply. The sound of her laughter echoing down the hall, the late-night talks, and even getting on her for leaving the bathroom counter messy. She wrapped her arms around me first, holding on longer than usual.

"I'll call when I land," she said, her voice a little shaky but trying to stay strong.

"You better," I whispered, brushing a strand of hair from her face. "And remember, I love you."

Then she turned to Guillermo. He opened his arms without a word, and she stepped into them. For a moment, neither of them said anything. When she finally pulled away, I caught the shimmer in Guillermo's eyes. He blinked fast, trying to will the tears away, but I saw the emotion on his face as clear as day.

"I'm proud of you, *mija*," he said softly.

The next time we'd see her would be at graduation, and that felt both far away and close.

Chapter 12

"La Negra Tiene Tumbao"

I was running late, and I had five minutes remaining before the exam began. Guillermo dropped me off at the front of the building. I rushed inside, heart pounding, nerves frayed. Security pointed me in the right direction, and I made my way to the testing room.

I handed the proctor my ID with my heart pounding, and with trembling fingers, I found a seat toward the back. I looked around, and the room was filled with others like me: determined, weary, and hopeful. I wrapped my hand around the pencil like it was my lifeline. There was so much at stake, and this wasn't just a test. It was proof I still dreamed that even as a mother, a wife, an immigrant starting over in a country that didn't always see me, I still had something to offer. I belonged in that room.

I steadied myself, closed my eyes for a moment, and began. I whispered a prayer to God and asked Santa Barbara to grant me the strength to guide my hand, clear my mind, and carry me through.

Four hours later, I was finally done. I handed my exam to the proctor, my fingers stiff from writing, my heart pounding with a mix of relief and exhaustion.

As I stepped outside, the cool air hit my face, and the tears came streaming. They weren't just tears of fatigue, though. It was a release. I was happy that Guillermo had not arrived as I needed a minute to be still, to let myself feel the weight of what I had just done. A reminder of how far I'd come, and how much I still carried.

As I stood outside wiping my face, I thought about the long nights studying, learning a new language, while the kids slept, the guilt of missing bedtime stories, and the doubts that crept in when I was alone. I thought about my mother, who never had this chance, and about all the women like her, women like me, who were told their dreams had an expiration date.

I beeped Guillermo to let him know that I was done. When he finally pulled up, he looked at me through the windshield and smiled.

"You okay?" he asked as I climbed in.

I nodded, my eyes still wet with tears. "I did it."

He handed me a beautiful bouquet of flowers, then leaned over and kissed me.

"Guillermo, you didn't have to buy me flowers."

"They're from me and the kids," he said gently.

That's when I broke down. They had seen the late nights, the sacrifices, and they knew I was doing it for them.

Guillermo didn't need to ask how it went. He simply reached over, squeezed my hand, and said, "I knew you would." And in that moment, beneath the soft hum of the engine, I let myself finally accept what life had in store for me.

****

Six weeks had come and gone. The anticipation leading up to receiving my letter from the State Boards felt like I was going to lose my mind. Then, finally, one Thursday afternoon, I found a letter in the mailbox wedged between a grocery flyer and an unpaid light bill. It was thin, too thin, I thought, and my heart sank.

I stood on the porch, keys still in hand, staring down at my name printed neatly on the front. For a moment, I couldn't move. All I could think was: What if I failed? What if all of it was for nothing?

Then I heard kids laughing inside, followed by the clatter of dishes and Guillermo's voice calling out for me. I took a breath.

Steady, I opened the envelope.

Congratulations.

That one word blurred as the tears welled in my eyes. I read it again, just to be sure. I passed.

I pressed the letter to my chest and whispered, *"Gracias."* To God. To Santa Barbara and to myself.

Inside, no one knew yet, but in that moment, standing alone on our worn wooden steps, I felt like I had climbed a mountain.

"Guillermo!" I called out.

"¡Voy!" he answered from the other room. He came around the corner, saw my face, and froze.

"Is everything okay?" he asked.

I handed him the letter, unable to speak. His eyes scanned the page, and then, beaming, he shouted, *"¡Pasaste el examen!"* He lifted me off the ground in one swift motion, spinning me around like we were twenty again. I laughed through tears, the letter still in my hand.

The commotion brought the kids running. "What happened?" Antonio asked, eyes wide.

"Your mamá passed her exam!" Guillermo announced, grinning like a proud schoolboy.

Carolina squealed and threw her arms around my waist, while Antonio danced around us, feeding off the joy in the room.

At that moment, I wasn't just a wife, or a mother, or an immigrant woman trying to make it. I was someone who had dared to dream again and won.

Guillermo looked at me, his eyes soft. *"Te lo dije—*you could do this." And for the first time in a long while, I didn't doubt it. I believed it too.

Later that night, after the kids had gone to bed, I sat at the kitchen table with a cup of warm tea, the envelope resting beside me like a companion.

Passing the exam was just the beginning. There were still applications, interviews, and the challenge of proving myself in rooms where my accent might speak before I did.

And yet, for the first time in years, I wasn't afraid. I reminded myself I was a nurse in Cuba. I had walked through fire to get here, and I was carving out something for myself.

It wasn't just about work. It was about dignity. About reclaiming the parts of me that had been stretched too thin.

Guillermo came in and placed a hand on my shoulder. "What are you doing?" he asked.

"Just thinking about what's next," I replied.

He smiled. "You've got this. There's nothing to worry about. You have the experience. You're ready."

"You're right, Guillermo."

He leaned in, his voice low and playful. "Then let's go celebrate…in the room." I burst out laughing as I stood up to follow him, the weight of the day finally giving way to joy.

With my license finally in hand, I could breathe and, for the first time in years, take a trip just for us.

****

Guillermo loaded up the station wagon as we got ready to head to Miami for Karime's high school graduation. He was out of school for a few weeks before summer classes started, and I had taken some vacation time from the diner. Once we returned, I would begin my job search as a nurse.

Thankfully, the school counselor had offered to help guide me through the process. She encouraged me to take this time off with the family, reminding me that once I start working, my schedule would change. Besides, I needed the time to just relax and spend time with Guillermo and the kids.

I cooked and packed all our food and drinks for the trip, carefully tucking everything into the cooler and arranging it next to the suitcases in the trunk. It was our first real family vacation, just the four of us. Excitement buzzed in the air, mingling with the scent of roasted chicken, Congri, Yucca, and homemade pastelitos de queso y guayaba straight from the oven wrapped in foil. Antonio and Carolina had brought along their blankets and pillows and their favorite snacks. Antonio was growing so fast that Guillermo had to adjust the space in the back to make room for his long legs.

After filling up the tank, we hit the interstate. I glanced back at my kids, slouched in their seats, headphones on, eyes fixed on the road ahead. They were changing right before our eyes, not just growing up, but being shaped by a world that didn't always know what to make of them.

They proudly identified as Cuban, yet they often wrestled with the complexities of that identity, especially in how others saw them. Because of the color of their skin, they were sometimes made to feel like they weren't "Latino enough" in Latino spaces, and not "Black enough" in Black ones. It was a painful tightrope to walk, one that left them often feeling unseen and unheard.

I could see it in the questions they asked, the stories they didn't want to tell. Once, Antonio told me how a classmate asked if he was "really Cuban." Antonio would come home with stories frustrated, some were absurd. He'd recount moments when elderly white Latina women would clutch their purses as he walked by, whispering about him in Spanish, assuming he couldn't understand. Most of the time, he wouldn't say anything, choosing not to be disrespectful just as Guillermo and I had taught him. But every now and then, he'd respond with humor, saying *"con permiso"* or offering a friendly *"buenas tardes"* in perfect Spanish. Their eyes would widen in shock. Some would stumble over their words, asking awkwardly, *"¿Cómo aprendiste a hablar tan bien el español?"* as if his fluency somehow disrupted their assumptions about my child.

As the years went by, Spanish became less present in our home. Though Guillermo and I encouraged them to speak it, our children often replied in English. We were torn because we were learning the English language at the same time. With the kids around, we had more opportunities to engage in English with them. We quickly realized, though, that the less noticeable your accent, the easier it was to acclimate, especially in professional settings. Over time, the children's accents began to soften, eventually becoming barely detectable.

It wasn't just language they were shedding, it was a form of cultural camouflaging or an occasional code switching. Nonetheless, Guillermo and I did our best to affirm who they were, while the world around them kept trying to box them in.

During our drive to Miami, we switched radio stations depending on which state we were passing through. The Spanish-language programs were usually tucked away on the AM dial, their signals faint and crackling with static. The kids had grown tired of salsa. What once made them dance now made them roll their eyes. These days, it was all about American pop music and hip-hop, especially for Antonio.

Though hip-hop had been around since the early '70s, it was gaining momentum in urban communities and in our home, it had fully taken root through Antonio. He walked around the house with his Walkman, headphones on, completely immersed. Now and then, I'd catch him rapping, bobbing his head to the pulsing beat, then launching into a rhythmic stream of poetic words. The wall in his room was plastered with posters torn from *Word Up! Magazine*, of people he mostly identified with, such as Rakim, KRS-One, Scott La Rock, Kool DJ Red Alert, Chuck Sugarhill Gang, RUN DMC, Special Ed, Public Enemy, Salt-N-Pepa, MC Lyte, MC Shan, Special Ed, and LL Cool J. He was captivated by the raw energy and storytelling in the music. Something about it spoke to him, echoing something deep and unspoken inside.

He would dance around the house, rapping, "*I'm talented, yes, I'm gifted. Never boosted, never shoplifted.*"

He even started dressing like the rap artists he admired. His haircut was a high top fade: asymmetrical tapered close on the sides, with the top higher and sloping upward. He wore Pan-African colors and cloth medallions around his neck, explaining that they were his alternative to the flashy gold chains we couldn't afford, but also a statement of pride and not just style.

I didn't say much at first, but I watched with concern. Antonio was still discovering who he was at sixteen, and lately, he had become deeply engrossed in Black nationalism. He began reading all kinds of material, some scholarly, others handed out in pamphlets on the street. It wasn't the scholarly texts that concerned me, though. It was the pamphlets, some of which were filled with anger and hate.

"Mom, I never forgot about the riots in Miami," he said one night, his voice low and steady. "For the longest time, I was angry about it. I still don't think people really understood what that kind of rage came from."

I stayed quiet, letting him speak.

"My disappointment came not only from the death of Mr. McDuffie," he continued. "It was everything being ignored, disrespected, profiled, teachers not understanding me. I remember how people looked at us in the store. Like we didn't belong."

I nodded in agreement, feeling the weight of his words settle deep in my chest. I had lived it too, we all had. Carolina, for instance, had started going by "Caroline" in school because that's what her teachers and classmates called her.

"That's not your name," I scolded gently.

She shrugged. "It's just easier, Mom."

"No," I said firmly. "You were named after *mi tía*, and there's power in your name. *Tu nombre es*, Caro-li-na. When they say it wrong, you correct them. *No me importa cuánto tiempo tome.* Eventually, they'll get it right."

It was important to me that Antonio learn our Cuban history, the struggles and the triumphs. But loving your people shouldn't mean rejecting everyone else. Guillermo and I reminded him who he was named after, a Cuban general, Antonio Maceo, known not only for his military brilliance, but for his unshakable commitment to justice and unity.

"Antonio Maceo fought for the liberation of all people in Cuba, regardless of race or class."

With excitement, Guillermo shared with Antonio a story he learned in school. "Antonio Maceo and his men rode on horses, swinging machetes like they were an extension of their own arms. The Spanish had guns, but Antonio Maceo didn't back down from this fight. He knew the terrain in eastern and central Cuba, and he used it to outsmart them at every turn. They couldn't catch him. He was fearless."

We told Antonio that true strength is knowing who you are and still choosing to embrace others. That freedom means nothing without compassion. Love for humanity, I told him, means love for the entire human race. At first, he didn't quite understand. It took time, and a few long conversations at the dinner table, but slowly, we began to see him reflect on those words. While we didn't want to pacify his observation on racism, we wanted him to feel heard, supported, and empowered to speak his truth without carrying the weight of it alone. The fire in my baby didn't dim, but it did start to burn with more purpose.

****

While we were on the road, Antonio woke up and said he wanted to talk to us about something. My stomach tightened. At his age, that could mean anything. Carolina was still sleeping, curled up with her pillow in the back seat.

"Yes, *dímelo*," I said, trying to keep my voice steady.

He hesitated for a moment, then got right to the point. "I want to go back to the high school in our neighborhood."

I turned slightly in my seat. "I thought you liked your school."

"I do," he replied quickly. "I like it."

"What about your teammates?" I asked.

He shrugged. "I think I have a better shot at going to the state championship if I transfer back to the school in our district."

The high school in our neighborhood had recently turned a corner. It used to be in the headlines for all the wrong reasons, mostly gun violence and low test scores, but things had changed. A new coach had come in, the academic support team was stronger, and there was a renewed sense of pride in the community. Students were returning, and the basketball program was starting to get statewide attention.

"There are more opportunities for you at your current school," I said gently. "Don't you want to go to college?"

"Yes and no."

"What do you mean?"

"I've been thinking about joining the army," he said. "They can pay for college. You know, Mom, 'Be All You Can Be.' You've seen the commercials."

"You could also earn a scholarship for playing sports," I reminded him.

Guillermo looked at me, then spoke carefully. "We understand wanting a plan, Antonio. But that path isn't easy. It's not just commercials and promises. You have to be sure."

"I know," he said, "but I don't want to put the burden on you and Mom. College is expensive."

I reached back and touched his arm. "*Mijo*, we never see you as a burden. We want you to dream big, and we're here to help you figure out how to make those dreams happen. Whether that's sports, college, or even the army, what matters most is that it's truly what you want."

He nodded slowly, in agreement, his eyes cast toward the window as the scenery rushed by. "I'm just trying to make the right move."

"You will," Guillermo said. "But don't rush it. Let's talk to the coach, look at your options. We'll figure it out together."

"The coach wants to meet with you guys when we get back," Antonio added.

Guillermo kept his eyes on the road but nodded. "Well, Antonio, we're not promising anything, but we'll listen. We just want to make sure you're making the right decision."

Antonio leaned back again, headphones in hand, and this time when he settled into his seat, there was something different in his posture. Not just rest but relief.

****

As we neared Miami city limits, the skyline began to rise in the distance, shimmering in the late afternoon haze. The palm trees grew taller, the traffic heavier, and the air hotter, thicker, almost with a kind of electric anticipation. It had been years since we'd all come to Miami together.

We exited the interstate and made our way through familiar streets, past pastel-colored buildings and neighborhood cafés with

Cuban music spilling out onto the sidewalks. Each turn stirred memories, the McDuffie riots, the boarded-up buildings. Not much had changed, except for a few new storefronts. The frustration of the residents hadn't changed much either, judging by the expressions on their faces. I was amazed there had been no rebuilding with the exception of a few stores.

When we finally pulled up to mi tía's house, the front door swung open before we even parked. She stood on the porch, arms wide, her eyes shining just as I remembered her: bright, fierce, and full of love.

"*¡Llegaron!*" she called out. "*¡Mi familia!*"

And just like that, we were home.

Chapter 13

"Quimbara"

We sat on the edge of our seats, waiting for Karime's name to be called. From afar, we spotted her in her cap and gown, seated among the other graduates, a small figure in a sea of hopeful faces. On stage, the principal and school staff stood ready, handing out diplomas one by one. Every so often, Karime would turn and wave, trying to catch our eyes. Guillermo was snapping photos nonstop, but I'd come prepared. We weren't going to miss a single moment of this special day.

Then they called her name. Karime Olivia Martinez. Watching her walk across that stage felt like a full-circle moment. Karime had worked so hard to get there, and we had all walked that journey with her. Guillermo and I, along with Carolina and Antonio, screamed with everything we had. Yasmine, Pedro, *mi tía*, and her son-in-law and daughter cheered beside us, all of us overflowing with pride. Yasmine's daughter was among the graduates, and we screamed for her when her name was called as well.

Later that day, Yasmine and Pedro hosted a barbecue at their home in honor of Karime and their daughter, Elba. People strolled through the yard dressed in black, handing out traditional Cuban hor d'oeuvres and drinks. A DJ spun a lively mix of rock, salsa and hip hop, giving the party an eclectic energy.

I looked across the yard and spotted Antonio, surrounded by a group of girls, clearly enjoying the attention. Carolina was in the pool, laughing with her cousin, both of them splashing and shrieking with delight.

Guillermo and I finally had the chance to meet Jeremy. He was clearly nervous, and we had promised Karime we wouldn't embarrass her. Jeremy was tall, with smooth, creamy-looking chocolate skin, a striking resemblance to Guillermo in his younger days. He was soft-spoken and shy, but thoughtful and polite.

"So, what are your plans for college?" Guillermo asked, gently breaking the ice.

"I'm going to Harvard. Same as Karime," Jeremy said, stealing a quick glance at her with a smile.

I was happy that Karime got a full four-year ride scholarship at Harvard. We were so excited to know that the financial burden would be lifted from us.

"Well, that's good," Guillermo replied. "At least she'll know someone."

Jeremy nodded. "Yes."

"And what are you planning to study?"

"Pre-med," he said softly.

"I'm a nurse," I added.

"Yes, Karime told me you passed the state boards. Congratulations."

"Thank you," I said with a smile.

It was clear Karime was growing restless, ready for us to wrap up the conversation, so we did. "Well, it was nice meeting you," I said. Guillermo shook Jeremy's hand, and the two of them walked off together, Karime looking relieved.

"So, what do you think?" I asked Guillermo.

"I like him for her. He seems kind. Respectful."

"Did you have a talk with her?"

"The talk?" he asked, raising an eyebrow. "Oh. Isn't that your job with the daughters?"

I laughed. "Yes, I suppose it is, and she told me they're taking things slow, but if anything happens, she'll be careful."

Guillermo let out a sigh of relief, and just then, the DJ switched to some old-school salsa classics we hadn't heard since leaving Cuba: Benny Moré, Celia Cruz, and others whose voices carried the soul of our island. Without a word, Guillermo and I stepped onto the dance floor like we owned it. Guillermo paused for a beat, chest lifted, one foot tapping to the rhythm, then rolled his shoulders with that signature swagger. He reached for my hand, and I spun into him, our bodies locking into a familiar groove. His hips circled in time with the congas, mine answering with the slow, sensual sway of the rumba. The music pulled us in, and soon a circle formed around us, everyone clapping and cheering. After a few songs, Guillermo extended his hand to *mi tía*, and the two of them danced for most of the night, smiling like it was Cuba *antes*.

As the evening wound down, Yasmine brewed a pot of *café*. Small shots of black coffee were handed out to everyone. We gathered around, chatting about the economy and swapping stories about Cuba *antes de la Revolución*. Pedro invited Guillermo and the other men for some tobacco and to a game of dominoes. I caught the look of surprise on Guillermo's face, maybe even a little hesitant, but he went along with it, blending into the flow of the night.

Later that evening, Guillermo and I settled into one of the guest rooms at Yasmine and Pedro's house. The kids were still up, sprawled out on the floor, watching movies in the theater room. *Mi tía*, worn out from the dancing and laughter, had already gone to bed.

After I showered, the bathroom light cast a shadow onto the bedroom wall where Guillermo, sitting up in bed, waited for me. I rolled my hair carefully and tied a scarf around it. When I turned off the bathroom light, the glow from the pool outside spilled gently into the room, casting a shimmering reflection across the walls. My nightgown hung loose, past my ankles, flowing as I walked across the room, the fabric sheer enough for my silhouette to show through.

Guillermo watched me without saying a word, his eyes soft, almost reverent. I walked slowly toward the bed, the night air settling around us. The faint rustle of palm leaves could be heard outside the window.

"You look beautiful," he said quietly, his voice low and full of meaning.

I smiled, easing under the covers beside him. At that moment, we didn't need anything but the comfort of each other's presence.

As we lay in bed, Guillermo turned to me and said, "I'm so happy I chose you to be my wife and the mother of my children."

"Oh, thank you, babe," I replied, touched.

"No, seriously," he continued. "Our daughter is going to Harvard University, *La crème de la crème*. You can't get any better than that. I know that in my younger years, and my struggle with drugs, I didn't always value our relationship the way I should have. Looking back, I was still a boy in a man's body. I want you to know I'm sorry and I'm forever grateful for you."

"I love you, Guillermo," I whispered.

Lying there beside him, I thought about all we had weathered, the long nights, the sacrifices, the dreams we had quietly stitched together through the years. His words stayed with me, not just because they were kind, but because they were real. Hard-won. Honest.

It's easy to forget, in the thick of raising children and chasing stability, that love deepens not only in joyful moments, but in the ordinary and difficult ones too.

Guillermo pulled me closer to him, his touch gentle, his kiss filled with longing. There was no urgency, only pure tenderness between us. Our bodies intertwined, folding into one another with ease, moving in perfect rhythm. When we reached that peak, he gently called out my name. It felt as though time folded in on itself. We held on to each other, breathless, bound by a love that had only deepened over the years. We drifted off to sleep, with his heart wrapped around mine.

****

It was time to head back to New Jersey, though the kids begged to stay a little longer. Karime still had a month and a half before she was due at Harvard, and Elba, also part of Harvard's Class of 1989, was just as excited. Yasmine and Pedro reassured us it was fine; they'd fly the kids back in time for the start of school.

As much as I knew I'd miss them, the thought of having some alone time with Guillermo felt like a gift. After everything, we both needed that time—just the two of us.

One by one, the kids took turns hugging us goodbye. *Mi tía* looked heartbroken to see us go. As always, she packed us a mountain of food for the road enough to last a week.

"Drive safely, and don't forget to call me when you get home," she said, her voice tight with emotion.

"We will," I promised, giving her one last hug.

"*Cuídate*," she whispered.

****

Our trip home was memorable. Guillermo and I stopped a few times in the Carolinas to do some sightseeing before hitting the road again. When we returned home to New Jersey, we learned that the owner of the house had passed away and his estate was putting the property up for sale. We were asked if we wanted to place an offer, but we declined. It felt like a sign that maybe this was the right time for a new beginning. We refused to rent again, so we went on the hunt to find our home.

While we were house hunting, I worked closely with my counselor, who had lined up a few job interviews for me. The first two went reasonably well, but I was really counting on the third one to come through. It was a nursing position at a major hospital, and I felt confident because my counselor knew the hiring supervisor personally and had put in a good word for me. I also had recommendations from Yasmine and Pedro.

For the interview, I wore a tailored blue suit with a blue-and-white blouse and black heels. My curls, now past my shoulders, were holding up beautifully. I did my makeup using some Fashion Fair I had picked up in Miami for Karime's graduation. Karime, my unofficial wardrobe stylist, had chosen both her father's and my outfits for the ceremony. Over the phone, she'd coached me on exactly what to wear for the interview, down to the earrings.

Even from a distance, she had a way of taking care of me. It was touching, really, to see how our roles had begun to shift. I had spent so many years guiding her, dressing her, reassuring her. And now, here she was, offering me the same in return. Her confidence in me gave me a boost I didn't know I needed. As I stood in front of the mirror one last time, I smiled, knowing that Karime's fashionable expertise was responsible for choosing the very clothes I wore.

With Karime's voice in my head, I stepped out the door feeling confident. As I drove to the hospital, I rehearsed answers to potential questions, steadied my breathing, and tried to quell the nervous flutter in my stomach.

When I arrived, I took a deep breath before walking into the brightly lit lobby. The air smelled faintly of disinfectant. Nurses in scrubs moved briskly down the hallways, and the sound of hospital life surrounded me. I checked in at the front desk and took a seat, straightening out my skirt and clasping my hands in my lap.

It had been a long road to get here. But in that moment, dressed in an outfit chosen with love, guided by the daughter I raised, I felt prepared for whatever came next.

I waited in the lobby until a tall white woman with reddish-brown hair and an unusual accent arrived to escort me inside to meet the hiring supervisor.

When I entered the office, the smell of a lit Winston cigarette permeated the air like a stubborn memory. Throughout the entire interview, she smoked her cigarette. A petite Black woman in her mid to late fifties stood to greet me. She wore large, round eyeglasses, and her glossy curls were neatly styled and sat on her shoulders, the scent of hair gel subtly noticeable. As she rose, I noticed the back of her chair was damp from the oily gel in her hair.

The interview lasted about thirty minutes. Afterward, she gave me a tour of the hospital, introducing me to several members of the nursing staff and a few doctors. Before we finished, she asked how soon I could start. I told her I'd be ready by Monday.

She offered me the position on the spot with a competitive starting salary and the potential for raises through promotions or annual cost-of-living adjustments. I would be working in the labor and delivery unit, three twelve-hour shifts a week. The job came with full-time benefits, including health insurance, vacation time, and a pension. I was thrilled not just about the opportunity, but also because Guillermo and I could finally share the cost of health and life insurance. Until then, most of his paycheck had gone toward covering the entire family's plan through his employer. I couldn't wait to tell Guillermo about the job offer.

****

That same afternoon, a realtor called about showing us some properties, but none were in the neighborhoods we'd asked about. It felt like a constant tug-of-war with her. There were always excuses from her as to why we weren't able to view the houses we requested.

We began to suspect it wasn't just a misunderstanding. It was subtle, but clear: we were being steered away from certain areas because of our race. It was frustrating, knowing that decades after the Fair Housing Act of 1968, which made it illegal to discriminate based on race, color, religion, sex, or national origin, these barriers were still around, wreaking havoc. We weren't asking for favors, just fairness.

We decided to start looking for homes on our own, tired of being shown places that didn't reflect what we were looking for or who we were. Then, one afternoon, I stumbled across a beautiful house in a nearby suburb. The neighborhood immediately struck me. It was quaint, welcoming, and, importantly, racially diverse. It felt like a place where we could belong, where our kids wouldn't stand out for the wrong reasons.

I knocked on the door, and an elderly woman answered. After I introduced myself, she warmly invited me in. The house was two stories with all the bedrooms upstairs, a finished basement, a huge kitchen, a living room and dining room, a spacious backyard, and two and a half bathrooms. It had the kind of layout that invited family gatherings and relaxed evenings. She mentioned a ballpark figure for what they were thinking of selling it for, and I left feeling hopeful.

I went home and told Guillermo about the job offer and the house. I then brought him back to see the house. He loved it as much as I did. With the kids preparing to head off to college, we thought it could be a home they'd return to or even one they might inherit someday. We made an offer and closed thirty days later.

"Okay, come on out and make sure your eyes are closed," I said.

When the kids opened their eyes, they were in shock, but had questions.

We spent the rest of the afternoon exploring every inch of the house, opening closet doors, peeking into cabinets, and imagining where the furniture would go. Carolina picked the sunniest bedroom upstairs, already making plans to hang posters and fairy lights. Karime was excited that she wouldn't have to share a room with her sister when she came home. Antonio raced through the hallway, counting steps and testing the echo of his voice in the empty space.

Guillermo walked through each room slowly, almost reverently. "I can't wait to paint these walls. He paused by the kitchen window, watching the way the light fell onto the counter. "It feels so right," he said quietly.

I nodded in agreement. "It does."

There was something sacred on that first day in the new house. A kind of peace we hadn't felt in a long time. No moving boxes yet, no noise, no routine. We were finally settling down in a place to call our own.

Chapter 14

"Oye Como Va"

Over the years, Karime and Yasmine became inseparable. Their bond deepened in ways that sometimes left Guillermo and me feeling left out, wondering if Karime even needed us anymore. Yasmine slipped into our lives with grace, filling spaces we hadn't realized were empty. She bought Karime's school clothes and surprised her with a used car to help her get around Cambridge.

We were proud and grateful beyond words to see Karime so loved and supported. Yet beneath that gratitude, something unsettling stirred, an ache I struggled to name. I often caught myself wondering if Yasmine was simply better at being a mother than I was. After all, she could give Karime more than I ever could.

The practical worries were there, too: the cost of another car insurance policy, the plans we were already making to buy Antonio a car as his schedule grew more chaotic. Everything around us was changing, and no matter how tightly I tried to hold on, the truth was clear: it was time to start letting go.

And yet, I welcomed the support with all my heart. As her mom, I couldn't have been prouder or more grateful. *Mi tía* sent her a little money to help with expenses, and Guillermo and I added what we could. We spent an afternoon shopping with her, picking out linens, toiletries, and the little things that would make her dorm room feel less like a strange new world and more like a second home. Alberto and Isabelle, Carmen and Maya, each gave gifts with so much love and care. Every dollar, every gesture, felt like a small prayer for her success. It really does take a village to raise a child, and in those moments, I could see just how loved, supported, and surrounded Karime truly was. Watching her step into her new life, I realized we were all helping her carry the dreams we had once carried for ourselves.

Before we left the house, we had to undergo Karime's final wardrobe inspection; no one escaped it. "Mom, I like it when you wear your hair down, not pulled up in a ponytail," she said gently, smoothing a few stray curls with her hand. "Carolina, come here so I can fix your blouse."

Guillermo and Antonio had just come back from the barbershop, smelling like aftershave and looking fresh but still not quite ready in Karime's eyes. Antonio flat-out refused to change his clothes. His style had become a part of his identity, and Karime knew by now that trying to change him would only start a battle she wouldn't win. Guillermo, eager to please, changed without protest.

As I watched Karime fuss over all of us, a question gnawed at me: Was she proud of us, or was she trying to make us look like we belonged? Did we not measure up to the polished families she spent time with in Miami? I smiled through it, but the ache stayed with me.

When we pulled up to her dorm, the parking lot was filled with families unloading their cars, carrying suitcases and boxes toward the building. Cambridge was beautiful. Students strolled across the sprawling, manicured lawns, laughter and chatter filling the air. The dorm rooms were regular size and large enough to fit two people comfortably. We helped Karime organize her belongings. I even sprinkled holy water blessed by Father Ortega throughout the room to ward off any evil spirits.

Her pink comforter and pillows were arranged neatly on her bed with her alarm clock within reach, and the phone was on her nightstand. She also had a framed print of our family portrait we took at Sears Roebuck.

Karime's roommate, Susan, had already arrived with her parents and younger brother. They were from Columbus, Ohio and looked like the kind of all-American family you'd see in a Sunday newspaper ad for corn flakes cereal.

Susan was a petite white girl with long, ash-blonde hair and a warm, eager smile, almost too eager, like she was trying to make a good impression on everyone at once. Needless to say, Karime seemed to connect with her right away.

The evening was winding down, and the campus had mostly emptied. We knew it was time to go, though none of us were ready. Karime walked us to the car, her steps slowing with every few feet, as if trying to make the moment last just a little longer.

I fought back my tears, willing myself to stay composed for her. Beside me, Guillermo wiped at his eyes, blaming it on the breeze.

Antonio stepped forward first, pulling Karime into a hug. "I'm going to miss you, Sis," he whispered.

That was all it took. Carolina burst into tears, holding Karime tightly. Karime tried to be strong, but when she collapsed against Guillermo's chest, the sobs came in waves.

I reached for her, wanting to freeze the moment, knowing I couldn't.

When I looked at Karime, she wiped her tears and gave me a quick, brave smile, but I caught it: the slight quiver in her chin, the way she gripped my hand a second longer before letting go. She was trying to be strong for us, just as we were trying to be strong for her.

"My car arrives tomorrow," Karime said, trying to change the subject.

The mention of the car rattled my nerves.

"You be careful," I said quickly.

"I will, Mom," she promised.

"Yasmine, Pedro, and Elba arrive tomorrow," she added, "and Jeremy will be here tomorrow, too."

"Please give Yasmine, Pedro, Elba and Jeremy a hug and a kiss for me," I said, my voice catching. I realized that growing up wasn't just about her letting go of us; it was about us letting go of her, too.

We arrived home late from Cambridge. The kids were nearly asleep as we walked through the door, and everyone drifted off in different directions. Antonio disappeared into the basement with blankets in tow, Carolina headed upstairs to her room, and Guillermo jumped in the shower before going straight to bed.

While everyone was sleeping, I drew a long, hot bath and let my thoughts drift to Karime. Sometimes during my shifts at the hospital, when the doctors made their rounds, I found myself bragging about my future doctor, Karime. Their faces would light up with surprise and admiration, and for once, they looked at me differently, not as an immigrant they believed was trying to milk the system, but as someone who was in direct competition for a piece of the American pie. I still couldn't believe my baby was now a freshman at Harvard University.

After I lotioned my body and combed my hair, I slipped into bed and pressed myself against Guillermo, hoping he would catch the hint. But he was fast asleep, snoring softly, unreachable no matter how much I tried to wake him. Eventually, I surrendered to sleep, feeling a bit rejected, only to be awakened hours later by his touch.

He trailed slow kisses along my thighs before moving up to my breasts, his mouth gentle and familiar. He guided me to climb on top of him, and soon, our bodies moved together, finding their rhythm as naturally as breathing. When I cried out his name, I caught myself, my heart racing, hoping the kids hadn't heard.

It was a rainy Sunday, and thankfully, we had nowhere to be, and neither did the kids. With everyone's schedules so full, days like this felt like a blessing. Most of the time, I could barely keep up. On the days I worked, Guillermo handled the after-school shuttling. Antonio was busy with varsity basketball, often traveling for away games. Carolina was juggling cheerleading tryouts and debate team meetings. This day of rest meant more to me than I could put into words. After breakfast, everyone drifted back to their rooms. Guillermo and I stayed in bed, watching movies while dinner simmered slowly in the crockpot.

Guillermo, how about we call Karime?" I asked.

"You don't think it's too soon?" he said, half-smiling.

"No, not at all. I know we just left her, but… I want to hear her voice."

I picked up the phone and started calling her number. I heard Antonio yell that he was on the phone. Antonio was deep in conversation with one of his female friends.

"You have five minutes," I told him, cutting in. "I need to call your sister." Then I hung up before he could argue.

I dialed Karime's number, but there was no answer. A knot tightened in my stomach. I tried to shake it off, but the worry had already crept in.

"She's probably hanging out with her friends," Guillermo said.

"That's true."

Those anxieties eventually faded as the four years flew by in a blur of campus visits, late-night calls, and care packages stuffed with her favorite snacks and notes from home. Watching her and my other children grow into their own, I knew the worry would never fully disappear; it just changed. But so did my faith. I had to trust that we raised her right. Besides, we were entering a new season not just as parents, but as witnesses to our children's lives, learning to let them lead their own way.

Chapter 15

"Saludo a elegua"

Antonio enlisted in the Army and quickly rose through the ranks, becoming a Staff Sergeant. It had been six long years since we last saw him in person. He kept in touch the best he could: letters written in his neat handwriting, photos of him in uniform, standing beside desert landscapes or Army barracks. Each message felt like a lifeline, a small window into the life he was carving out far from home.

When Tía passed away, I sent a telegram to his base, uncertain if the news would reach him in time, or if duty would prevent him from coming back. We knew he fought in the Persian Gulf War. We didn't know if he would make it home. We didn't ask. We just waited.

On the day of the funeral, the small Catholic church overflowed with people dressed in all black, with women in elegant hats of every size and style. Mi tía lay lifeless in a purple dress, surrounded by bundles of red roses arranged lovingly around her mahogany casket.

It finally hit me that mi tía had gone to glory, and I would no longer be able to call her for advice or see her again. She was like a mom to me. Through her, I finally understood what it meant to be truly loved unconditionally by a mother. I missed her deeply already.

I had always known she was cherished within our family, but I hadn't realized just how many lives she had touched. Former neighbors, Yasmine and Pedro's friends, colleagues from work, and even former students all of them came to pay their respects. Her legacy filled every pew.

As the priest began the service, sunlight pierced through the vibrant stained-glass windows depicting the Virgin Mary and Jesus Christ. Suddenly, the church doors creaked open, and every head turned. There stood my son, Antonio Maceo, in full Army dress blues. A silence fell over the room. My heart caught in my chest. He walked slowly down the aisle, tall and composed, looking so much like his father. The broad shoulders. His strength. The kind that's earned, not inherited. Guillermo and I couldn't stop crying.

As Antonio sat beside me and gently placed his hand over mine. I whispered a silent thank you to God and *mi tía*, whose spirit I felt in that church. She would've smiled to see him come home, even just for a moment. Her blessings permeated the sanctuary like incense in the air.

After the service, mourners surrounded him and the family, thanking him for his service and sharing stories about Tía, how she had prayed for their families, helped them find work, or opened her door when no one else would. Her generosity had rippled far beyond what any of us knew.

Later that evening, we gathered at Yasmine and Pedro's home. We stayed up late talking, laughter and memories shared among us. I looked around and felt a sense of gratitude. Our children were now grown, Antonio recounting stories from his deployments, Karime reflecting on the intensity of her first year as a surgical resident at the University of Miami, and my youngest, Carolina, announcing her engagement with a huge rock on her finger. She was preparing to graduate from NYU with plans to live and work in the city with her fiancée, Mathew, who was Jewish and grew up in Westport, Connecticut.

I looked over at Guillermo, hoping he would find the courage to share his MS diagnosis with everyone, something the two of us had been dealing with for some time. When we first learned the news, I immediately called Yasmine. She spoke to his doctor, reviewed his labs, and reassured us that multiple sclerosis was no longer the death sentence it once was. With the right medication and a disciplined diet, she said, he could live a full life.

Two years into his diagnosis, Guillermo still didn't need a cane, and we counted that as a blessing. But there were days when his legs stiffened without warning, leaving him sore and unsteady. He rarely drove anymore. Most evenings, I'd pick him up from work, and we'd head home together. After dinner, we made it a point to walk—slow, steady laps around the neighborhood. It was our ritual. Our way of moving forward, one step at a time.

It was during those walks, beneath the street lamps and the soft rustle of trees, that we found our rhythm again. Sometimes we walked in silence, other times we talked about everything from his fatigue to my fears to the kids' futures. There was something healing about the routine of it. Guillermo would slide his arm around my shoulder, and even if his steps were slower, his presence was steady.

One night, as we paused near an old oak tree on the corner, he looked at me and said, "I may not move as fast as I used to, but I'm still walking beside you." We were up in age now, and my love for Guillermo never wavered. And he was in every sense what mattered to me and our children.

****

One day while visiting Florida again, Yasmine and I spent time on her patio near the pool, where we drank wine and allowed the nightly sky to comfort us with its calmness and beauty.

"How's Guillermo doing?" she asked gently.

"He's hanging in there," I said. "Some days are better than others."

She nodded. "Has he filed for disability yet?"

"No. He still wants to work. The school's been incredibly supportive, but…" I trailed off, unsure how to finish the thought.

"*Prima*," she said, placing her hand on mine, "you should start the process anyway. Disability can take time, and some people don't get approved on the first try. If things get harder later, at least you'll be one step ahead."

I nodded. "We've talked about it. Guillermo doesn't want to admit that things are changing, and he definitely doesn't want the kids to know. Not yet."

"Have you told them anything at all?"

"No. He thinks it's too much, especially since Tía passed. He wants to protect them."

"I understand," Yasmine said. "But I hope he reconsiders. The kids need to know. You can explain it in a way that makes sense to them. They're strong, just like you two."

"I'll talk to him again," I said, grateful for her clarity.

"I'm here if you need me."

I looked at her for a moment, her face softening. "How are you feeling?"

She exhaled. "You know…I was never prepared for her death.

"She lived to be ninety-five."

"I know. That's a blessing." She stared into her glass of wine. "Still, it hit me hard."

"I know. She was your confidant."

"I miss her so much."

"I do too."

"You know, Pedro and I are planning our retirement.

"Really?"

"Yes, *Prima*. It's time. My children and yours are adults. Now that *mi mama* is no longer here, I want to travel more. We are thinking about downsizing. This house is too big for just Pedro and me.

"Whatever you decide to do, I am here for you."

"Thank you."

There was a pause, full but comfortable. Then I turned to her. "Yasmine, I want to thank you for everything. For stepping in over the years, for being there for Karime, and for my whole family. I see the way you show up, and I don't take it for granted."

"My mom wouldn't have had it any other way," she said with a smile. "*¡Somos familia!* And honestly? Karime reminds me so much of myself. She's doing amazing work during her residency. I'm so proud of her."

Changing the conversation, Yasmine asked, "When is Carolina getting married?"

I laughed. "I don't even know. I'll probably find out the day before. She'll walk into the kitchen tomorrow and say, 'Mom, the ceremony is on Monday.' That's just how Carolina is."

"Remember her Quince?"

"Do I remember? Of course I do. Carolina refused to do the dance routine after she and her court had spent weeks rehearsing it! She was too shy to perform, but with a little convincing from Tia, she finally gave in. They did a fantastic job.

We both burst into laughter, the kind that spans years of fond memories.

I looked at Yasmine: my cousin, my sister and my friend and saw that her beauty hadn't faded. The silver strands threading through her mostly black hair wove through like threads of wisdom. One thing was clear: we weren't just mothers anymore. We were becoming the matriarchs now, the ones who hold the line, the ones others turned to. There was no ceremony to mark this change in our lives. No applause. Just knowing that crept in on nights like this, under the stars, with a glass of wine in hand and grown children living the lives we once only prayed for.

We had survived so many storms, storms of loss, illness, and uncertainty. And yet, here we were, still standing, still laughing, still loving.

****

Guillermo was already asleep when I slipped into bed. I hoped the sound of the shower and the rustling in the bathroom hadn't disturbed him. Lying there, I smiled, thinking about my conversation with Yasmine. For the first time, it felt like we connected in a way that went beyond family, but woman to woman, heart to heart. I think *mi tía* had a hand in that. Her spirit always had a way of pulling people closer when it mattered most.

But then my thoughts drifted to what Yasmine said about Guillermo. I knew she was right and that we needed to start the paperwork, to be prepared. But part of me did not want to admit how much things had already changed. It wasn't just the stiffness in his legs or how often I drove us home now. It was the smaller things. The moments we didn't talk about.

I hadn't told anyone, not even Yasmine, that Guillermo had been struggling to maintain his erections. At first, we both pretended it was nothing. Just stress. Just age. But I knew he was embarrassed. And truthfully, so was I. Not ashamed of him, but unsure of how to say it out loud. Unsure of what it meant for us. We still touched, still held each other close, but sometimes the silence after those failed moments felt heavier than words.

I stared up at the ceiling, listening to the soft rhythm of his breathing. He was still my husband. Still the love of my life. And yet I couldn't deny how afraid I was of what the future might ask of us or me.

But tonight, for the first time in a long time, I also felt ready to face it with honesty, with grace, and with help. We had always been stronger together.

Just as I began to drift off, I felt Guillermo stir beside me. He turned slowly, blinking awake.

"You okay?" he asked, his voice low and thick with sleep.

I hesitated. "Yeah. Just thinking."

He reached for my hand under the covers and gave it a gentle squeeze. "About earlier?"

I nodded in the dark, unsure how much to say.

A long pause followed, and then quietly he said, "I know I haven't been the same lately. I feel it too."

My throat tightened. I turned to face him. Even in the dim light, I could see the worry behind his eyes.

"You don't have to say anything," he continued, "but I know what's happening. And I hate it. I hate how it makes you look at me."

"I don't look at you any differently," I whispered. "I just… I didn't know how to bring it up."

He sighed, his breath catching slightly. "It's not just about sex. It's about feeling like a man. Feeling like myself."

"I know," I said, brushing my fingers against his face. "And I miss that part of us, too. But I miss it because I love you, not because I'm disappointed in you. Look, Guillermo, I love you the same way I did when we were younger. Nothing will ever change how I feel about you."

We lay there in the stillness, facing each other, nothing between us but truth.

"I want to talk to the doctor," he said finally. "Maybe there's something that can help. I don't want to pretend it's not happening."

"Okay," I said, tears streaming from my eyes. "Thank you."

It wasn't a solution, but it was a start, and that's all I had hoped for.

****

The next morning, we sat around the dining table, each of us wrapped in our own thoughts. Sunlight peeked through the blinds, softening the emotional weight of losing *mi tia*. A woman and a man, both dressed in crisp, neutral uniforms, moved through the room, placing plates in front of each guest. In the center of the table sat a beautiful arrangement of fresh flowers.

The conversation buzzed lightly around the table as everyone admired the presentation of the food. Yasmine, calm and gracious as always, gave her staff instructions to bring out more ice water and fresh lemonade.

Guillermo stirred his cafe slowly. "I think it's time," he said, not looking up. "We need to tell the kids."

He looked at me then, his eyes filled with something between resolve and fear. "How do we even start that conversation?"

Once everyone was seated and the waitstaff had handed out the plates, Guillermo cleared his throat. "We wanted to talk to you all about something important."

The movement in the room became paralyzed. Everyone started looking around to see if anyone knew what he was about to say.

Guillermo glanced at me, and I gave him a small nod.

"I've been diagnosed with multiple sclerosis," Guillermo said. "It's been a little over two years. I didn't want to tell you until I understood what we were dealing with."

No one spoke at first. Karime's eyes widened, her professional instincts kicking in. Antonio leaned forward, brows furrowed. Carolina reached for Mathew's hand under the table.

Karime leaned in, her tone sharp but loving. "What's your treatment plan? Are you seeing a specialist?"

Guillermo nodded. "Yasmine helped early on. I'm on medication. Most days, I'm okay."

Antonio exhaled. "How bad is it?"

"It's manageable. I don't drive much. My legs get stiff. But I'm still here. Still working. Still me. I didn't want to say anything until I had a better understanding of what we were dealing with," Guillermo continued. "I didn't want to worry anyone, especially while you were all starting your own lives. But it's time you knew."

Yasmine spoke gently. "I reviewed his lab work and had a few specialists at UM take a look. They said the condition is manageable—for now. They couldn't say how quickly it would progress over time. With the right medication and a disciplined diet, it can be controlled, reducing the chances of complications.

"I don't know what to say," Carolina whispered. "Why didn't you tell us sooner?"

I reached across the table and took her hand. "Because we were scared. And honestly, we didn't want this diagnosis to take up space in your lives when you were just beginning to live them."

"But we're not kids anymore," Antonio said softly. "We're your family. Let us carry some of this weight with you."

Guillermo's eyes glistened. "That's all I've ever hoped for."

"Papi, I have a lot of vacation time saved," Karime added. "I'm going to spend some of it in New Jersey with you and Mom. I want to go with you to your next doctor's appointment."

She stood and walked over, wrapping her arms around him. "We're in this together, Papi. Whatever you need." She kissed him on the cheek.

Carolina followed, eyes full of tears, while Antonio reached across the table and gripped his father's hand.

"I'm going to talk to my commander," Antonio said. "See if I can extend my leave by a month. Just in case."

"I just finished finals," Carolina chimed in. "I can stay a bit longer, too."

Yasmine nodded. "The holidays are coming up in a few weeks. This way, everyone can spend it together in New Jersey. And I think it's a great idea," she added. "It gives you all some extra time to rearrange your schedules."

"Good idea," Carolina agreed with a smile.

Guillermo shook his head, moved. "I don't want you changing your lives or plans for me. Your mom and I have this under control," he said tearfully.

"You'd do it for us," Antonio said.

As we continued to eat, the heaviness from his diagnosis started to lift slightly, especially now that the kids knew about his condition. We were no longer hiding from the truth. As a family, we were facing this debilitating disease head-on.

Now that the family knew about Guillermo's diagnosis, I noticed a change in him. He seemed more upbeat, more like himself again. During our flight home, we reflected on our time in Miami.

"I miss *mi tia* already," I said.

"I am going to miss her, too."

Guillermo stared out the window, captivated by the ocean blue sky and the clouds that looked like soft mountains drifting by.

"Rosita, the clouds are beautiful," he said quietly. "I wonder if Guillo knows about my illness."

"I'm sure he does," I replied. "He just wants you to rest and not worry. That's his way of showing love."

As soon as we arrived home, Antonio called in to check on us. He told us the good news that his commander signed off on his coming home for the holidays.

"I can't wait to see you, too, Antonio," Guillermo said. One by one, they were calling to speak to their dad. Yasmine called as well. We were so happy to know that all of us would be home for the holidays.

That evening, I lit a white candle at my altar and whispered a prayer to Eleguá. He who opens doors. He who guards the crossroads. I asked him to clear the path ahead for Guillermo, and to help me walk it with courage."

****

While I was showering, I felt Guillermo step in behind me. He wrapped his arms around my waist, and for a moment, we just stood there under the hot, steamy water. Slowly, we began to wash each other, his hands moving with care and tenderness, like he was learning my body all over again. Steam rose around us, wrapping us in a private world mingled between comfort and desire.

We kissed, soft at first, then deeper like we were reminding each other of something we hadn't said out loud in a while. Without a word, we stepped out and made our way into the bedroom. Guillermo opened the dresser drawer and reached for something only we knew about *la luz roja*.

It was a red light bulb he used to buy for the kids' Halloween parties, back when they were little and the house was filled with scary monsters, fairy costumes and candy. But over time, it became our secret. He once screwed it into the bedside lamp just to be silly, and we laughed until we cried. But that night, something shifted. The light cast a soft crimson glow across the room, and we discovered what it could do for us. Since then, whenever that red light came on, it meant everything was on pause, and it was just us.

He changed the bulb and switched on the clock radio. The crackle of static gave way to the smooth sound of L.T.D.'s "Love Ballad," pouring from the speakers like an invitation to dance.

Guillermo reached for my hand, and I placed mine in his. Then, as if on cue, the next song began with our song, Billy Joel's "Just the Way You Are." Guillermo closed his eyes and smiled.

From then on, we didn't speak. We didn't need to.

He pulled me close, with his hands on my waist, my arms around his neck, gently guiding me. We slow-danced right there in our bedroom, swaying to the music, barefoot on the hardwood floor. Time melted. The years, the kids, the stress, the diagnosis, none of it mattered in that moment. It was just two people, deeply in love, still choosing each other over everything.

We danced long after the song faded, as one melody melted into the next, each one echoing what the first had already stirred in us. We were so in sync, so attuned to each other, nothing could break this romantic spell.

My cheek rested against his chest, his breath warm against my hair. The hardwood floor creaked beneath our feet like it remembered the weight of our shared years. But tonight wasn't about memory. It was about presence. We were still choosing. Still loving.

Chapter 16

"Déjame Vivir"

Carolina met me for lunch at a charming tavern just outside of Paterson, looking every bit like a beautiful pop star. She strolled in fashionably late, dressed head to toe in designer labels. Her shoulder-length hair was tousled with loose curls that partially hid the oversized hoops on her ears and grazed her neck. She wore a black leather jacket over a lacy black crop top, paired with fitted jeans and sleek black combat boots. Colorful bracelets were stacked along her wrists and arms, adding a splash of boldness to her look.

All eyes followed her as she walked toward our booth and leaned in to kiss my cheek.

"Hi, Mami. I'm so sorry I'm late—traffic in the city was horrible."

"That's okay. You're here now and you're safe.

"How's Papi?"

"He's doing well. Still working. Antonio sent him some airplane models to assemble. You know your father, the engineer in him couldn't resist. Keeps him busy on the weekends."

Carolina smiled as she slid into the booth. "That sounds like my big brother Antonio. He's always been thoughtful."

"He really is," I said, pouring her a glass of water from the carafe. "They talk almost every week. It lights your father up."

A server approached us to take our order, and after a few quick glances at the menu, we both settled on salads and a shared appetizer.

As soon as the server walked away, Carolina leaned in. "I've been meaning to ask…how are you? Really."

I hesitated, touched. "I'm good, *mija*. Tired sometimes, but grateful. Things feel better lately. I've learned to appreciate that."

She reached for my hand across the table. "You've always carried so much. I just want to make sure you're taking care of yourself, too."

"I'm learning. Slowly. But seeing you like this, thriving—it reminds me that all the hard days were worth it."

Her eyes welled. "Whenever someone compliments me on my confidence or drive, I think of you. You gave me the blueprint."

"Thank you, baby. It comes with life experiences."

"No, really, Mami. I've always admired your strength. I just hope I can be half the woman you are."

"You will be."

Just then, the server returned with our food, and we both smiled politely as he placed the plates in front of us.

Carolina took a breath, her fork hovering above her salad. "I don't know how to say this…but I've been having second thoughts about getting married."

I looked up, concerned. "Why?"

"He wants to start a family right away, and I still want to travel. His views are more conservative than mine. Sometimes I feel like we're living in two entirely different futures."

"Have you told him how you feel?"

"I've tried," she said. "He doesn't really listen. It's like he's already decided for both of us."

Carolina's cheeks flushed red, her breathing sharp and uneven. It was the same look she had as a child when anger or fear took over.

"Carolina, *cálmate*. Here, drink some water," I said softly.

"I'm okay, Mom. I'm just anxious."

I reached across the table, laying my hand gently over hers. She squeezed back, a silent reminder that even in her storm, she knew I was there for her.

"Marriage isn't a box you check. It's a choice, one you make daily. Both people need to feel heard. Especially about matters that are important."

She nodded, wiping her eyes. "I just don't want to disappoint anyone. His family's already making plans, and part of me thinks maybe I should just go along with it."

"Go along with it, but not at the cost of your peace. If he can't hear you now, how will he hear you later when things get harder?"

She stared down at her plate. "I keep wondering if love is supposed to feel this heavy."

"Love can be hard, but it shouldn't make you feel like you're disappearing. It's not supposed to feel like losing yourself."

She wiped the corner of her eye. "Do you think I'm making a mistake?" Carolina opened her makeup compact to see the condition of her face after crying.

"I think the mistake would be pretending you're okay when you're not. You owe it to yourself and to Matthew to be honest."

Then she took a deep breath and said, "I think I needed to hear that."

"I think you already knew it. You just needed someone to remind you."

Carolina leaned back against the booth, exhaling slowly like a weight had been lifted, if only slightly.

"I haven't told anyone else," she admitted. "Not even my friends. Everyone just assumes I'm happy, but I've been waking up in the middle of the night, anxious. Like I'm trying to convince myself this is the right thing."

"You don't need to convince yourself of anything," I said. "You already know how you feel. Now it's about being honest with yourself and with him."

She nodded, wiping the corner of her eye. "I think I need to press pause. Just take some time to really think. I love him, I do… But I need to love myself enough to be honest."

"That's not selfish, Carolina. That's wise."

She reached for her glass of water, her hands steadier now. "Do you think you and Papi rushed into marriage?"

I smiled, a little sadly. "We didn't just rush, we leapt, thinking love was enough to catch us. And maybe it was, for a while. If I had the chance to do it over, I would've asked more questions. Of myself. I would've demanded more respect."

Carolina looked at me, eyes softer now. "I don't want to live with regret."

"Then don't," I said gently. "Start with the truth. Whatever happens next, you deserve a life that fits you—not one you're squeezing into."

She nodded, more sure of herself now than when she walked in. "Thank you, Mami. I didn't come here expecting all this, but…I think I know what I have to do."

"I know you do."

We stayed for a while, our meals mostly untouched. Carolina hugged me, then climbed into her BMW and headed back to the city. I worried about her. I worried about Matthew's reaction to her wanting to end the engagement. Would he finally listen, or would he try to pressure her into continuing with wedding plans she no longer wanted? Mostly, I felt guilty. I hadn't been the example she needed, and neither had Guillermo.

I prayed that she made the right decision.

When I came home, I found Guillermo in the backyard, tinkering with the lawn mower again, half-distracted by the game playing on the radio. He looked up when he saw me, his brow damp with sweat, that familiar smile tugging at his lips.

"Everything okay with Carolina?" he asked, wiping his hands on a rag.

"She's figuring some things out," I said, careful with my words. "She's not sure the life she's heading toward is the one she actually wants."

He nodded slowly, thoughtful. "It takes courage to admit that."

"It does," I said, folding my arms. "She's braver than I was at her age."

Guillermo looked at me then, not with judgment, but with something softer. Maybe it was understanding. Maybe it was regret.

"You were brave," he said. "You just didn't have anyone telling you it was okay to change your mind."

I didn't respond right away. I just looked at him, this man who had both broken my heart and held it together in different seasons. We had built something together, flawed and beautiful, messy and enduring. But we weren't always the best model of love. And deep down, I think we both knew that.

"She's watching us, you know," I finally said. "Even now. Even as a grown woman."

"I know," he said.

I nodded. "I'll give her a call later this evening to see how she's doing."

The cicadas buzzed in the trees. The air was heavy, but not unbearable. For once, I didn't rush to fill the moment. I let it be what it was: unfinished, uncertain, real.

****

That evening, I overheard Guillermo on the phone with Carolina.

"Your mom told me," he said, voice thick with emotion. "*Oye, mi princesa*—you deserve the best. Your mom and I… We were too young. I wasn't ready for the responsibility."

I leaned quietly against the wall, just out of sight.

"I thought love was enough," he continued. "I didn't know what love meant. Not really."

Carolina's voice came through, soft but clear. "I appreciate you saying that, Papi."

"I've made a lot of mistakes in life," he said. "But you—you're my greatest blessing. Don't let my failures make you settle. Not for anyone."

"I think I've been afraid of letting people down."

"You don't owe anyone your peace. Not even me."

I felt something loosen in my chest. For all we'd been through, we were still parenting her, still getting some of it right.

"I'm proud of you, Carolina," he added softly. "I don't say that enough. I love you."

"I love you too, *y Gracias*, Papi," she whispered. "I needed to hear that."

They said their goodbyes, and the call ended. Guillermo sat for a moment longer, staring at the phone in his hand.

I stepped into the room, and when he looked up at me, I didn't say anything right away. I just walked over and kissed his cheek.

"That was good," I said. "You were good."

He nodded, eyes a little glassy. "She's strong, Rosa. Stronger than we were."

I smiled. "Maybe. Or maybe she's just had a better example than we realized."

Later that weekend, Carolina stayed with us. She helped me reorganize my closet, and while sifting through scarves and shoes, I pulled out a photo from her First Communion.

"Look at this," I said. "You were so cute. Look at my baby."

She squinted at it and laughed. "Oh, Mami… I look mad."

"You were tired."

We laughed together, and that night, over dinner, she finally said it. "Mathew and I broke up."

Guillermo and I looked at her without shock. We just paid attention.

"I took your advice," she said. "It was time to put myself first."

"How did he take it?" Guillermo asked.

"We cried. But honestly? He wasn't ready either. He just didn't know how to tell me."

"How do you feel?"

"Relieved. Free."

I smiled. She had taken her step toward putting herself first.

After dinner, Carolina helped me clear the table, humming softly as she rinsed dishes at the sink. There was a lightness to her that I hadn't seen in weeks, maybe months. She moved with ease, like someone who had finally let go of something she'd been holding too tightly.

That night, after she went to her room to call a friend, I stood alone in the kitchen, wiping down the counters. Guillermo walked by and kissed the top of my head.

"You raised a strong one," he said.

I nodded. Because the truth was, I felt everything at once. Pride. Gratitude and pain. Carolina had done what I couldn't at her age; she listened to her gut and honored it.

I walked to the window. Outside, the porch light bathed the yard in a warm glow. I thought of myself in Cuba, young and barefoot, belly swollen with Karime, still dreaming of what my life might become. I didn't have the words then, but maybe, just maybe, I passed down the courage.

I closed my eyes, exhaled, and said a prayer for the woman my daughter was becoming, and for the parts of me she carried forward… A little braver, a little freer.

Chapter 17

"Gracias A La Vida"

I signed up for a lot of overtime. The holidays were approaching, and I wanted to pay down some of our credit cards before the new year. In America, good credit wasn't just a number; it was a lifeline. Without it, doors stayed closed. Apartments, home ownership, car loans. Even the ability to put something on layaway depended on a system we were taught to navigate the hard way. I didn't grow up thinking about credit scores, but here, it felt like a silent judge in every room, deciding what kind of life we were allowed to have. So we worked. Even when my body was tired, even when I missed dinner with the kids, I worked, because stability wasn't just a dream, it was something I had to earn hour by hour.

One evening at work, my supervisor called me into her office. My stomach dropped. I was sure I had done something wrong or was about to be fired.

I knocked gently on her door.

"Come in," she said.

I whispered a prayer before turning the knob, unsure of what to expect. As I stepped inside, the thick smell of cigarette smoke hit me instantly, clinging to the walls like wallpaper.

"You were looking for me?"

"Yes," she said, gesturing toward the chair across from her. "Please, have a seat."

Papers were scattered across her desk, and her computer monitor oversized and humming seemed to swallow what little space was left. She shuffled a few folders, still not looking up. Then she finally did, and her eyes appeared tired.

"I wanted to speak with you about something, but first, let me say you're not in trouble."

I let out a breath I hadn't realized I was holding.

"You've been working a lot of overtime," she continued. "Always on time. No complaints. Patients like you. The other nurses and the doctors respect you."

I nodded, still unsure where this was going.

"We have an opening in the ICU. It's more responsibility and more pay. I think you'd be a good fit."

Her words echoed in my mind. It was finally happening. For a moment, I said nothing. I just stared at her, making sure I had heard correctly.

"It's a demanding unit, but I've watched how you handle pressure. You're calm, compassionate, and sharp. You're exactly what we need."

"I… I'd be honored," I said once my voice returned. This was something I had always wanted. I was up for the challenge. Finally, my dreams were being realized and working in the ICU was exactly what I had prayed for.

She smiled, pulling a packet from under the pile of papers. "Take this home. Read it over. Let me know by the end of the week."

I left her office feeling better than I had in months. Not because I was finally being seen, but because, for once, I saw myself differently, too.

When I got home that night, Guillermo was in the kitchen, rinsing out a pot. I hung up my coat, still holding the packet in my hand like it might float away if I let go.

"You're home late," he said without turning around.

"Yeah," I replied, setting my purse down. "My supervisor asked to see me before I left."

He turned then, wiping his hands on a dish towel, with a concerned look taking over his face. "Everything okay?"

I nodded, then held up the folder. "She offered me a promotion. ICU. My hours would go back to working three twelve-hour shifts, but with more pay."

Guillermo raised his eyebrows. "ICU, huh? That's huge."

"It is," I said softly. "She said I was calm under pressure. That I had the right temperament for the job. The position doesn't start until January.

He walked over, took the packet from my hand, and looked at it like it was a certificate or a ticket to something.

"I'm proud of you," he said. "You've been working hard. You deserve this."

I smiled, but part of me still waited for the other shoe to drop— for him to ask how it would affect the house and him. But he didn't.

Instead, he leaned against the counter and said, "We'll figure it out. If this is what you want, we'll make it work."

He paused, then added, "I have some news too."

Dimelo.

"My supervisor asked me if I was ready to retire. The compensation package they offered is a decent one." He handed me an envelope, neatly folded, outlining his projected monthly income at different retirement ages. The longer he stayed, the higher the payout. The package also included full medical coverage and other incentives, plus eligibility for Social Security.

Still, I could see the weight behind his eyes. Every time the topic of retirement came up, Guillermo seemed to retreat inward. He couldn't shake the feeling that his MS was the real reason they were bringing it up. And no matter how generous the offer, it felt like he was being pushed aside. The truth was, the principal and staff adored him that couldn't have been further from the truth.

"So, what do you think?" I asked gently.

"I'm not ready to retire," he said. "I still have a few good years in me."

"If it's finances you're worried about, we'll be okay," I reassured him. "The money Tía left us, I placed in an IRA. It's gaining interest every year. We also have sizable equity from the house. We'll be fine."

Guillermo nodded slowly, but I could see the uncertainty in his eyes. "It's not just about the money," he said after a moment. "It's about feeling useful. Needed. I've been working since I was sixteen. What happens when I stop?"

I reached for his hand and wove my fingers through his. "You don't stop being needed just because you're not clocking in."

He looked at me, his voice low. "I know. But it's different now. My body… It doesn't always do what I ask of it. And when people at work start treating you like you're fragile, it's hard not to start believing it."

My heart ached hearing him say it out loud. The man who once carried this whole family on his back was now struggling with the weight of feeling left behind.

"You're still the heart of this family," I said. "Our kids respect you. I respect you. Your MS doesn't define you, and retirement won't erase everything you've built."

He didn't answer right away, just looked down at our hands, his thumb brushing gently over mine. "I just don't want to feel like I'm invisible," he said finally.

"You're not," I whispered. "We all see you."

He let out a soft laugh. "You always know how to say it better than I can."

I squeezed his hand. "That's what we do. We help each other find the words when they're too heavy to carry alone."

****

The idea of retirement became real the day Guillermo fell at home. Even though we weren't ready, life was making the decision for us.

It wasn't the first time, but this time felt different, more urgent. I had been calling him all morning, and when he didn't answer, a deep unease settled over me. I told my supervisor I had an emergency and left work immediately. When I walked through the door and found him on the kitchen floor, my heart dropped. He was conscious, but dazed and bruised. Thankfully, there were no broken bones, but still, the fall shook us both.

The kids were calling nearly every hour after we alerted them, each one trying to hide their panic. I did my best to stay calm, to reassure them their father would be okay, even as I struggled to process it myself. The doctor decided to keep Guillermo in the hospital for a few days for observation. It was the right call.

Carolina rushed to her father's side like the little girl who used to run into his arms after school. I watched him sleep, and I realized how the roles were changing. I wasn't just his wife; I was his caretaker now. And while I knew he wasn't ready to let go of work, maybe it was time we started preparing for a different season of our lives, one that required more patience, more presence, and more grace.

When Guillermo came home from the hospital, we tried to ease back into a routine, but everything felt more fragile. He moved a little slower, slept a little longer, and I noticed how he winced when standing up too quickly. Even though he brushed it off, I saw it. So did the kids.

Carolina stayed with us for a few days, helping around the house and gently nudging her father to rest. Antonio called during one evening and, in his usual way, got straight to the point. "Ma, is Papi going to retire now?"

I paused, unsure how to answer. We hadn't talked about it openly, not since the fall.

Later that night, as Guillermo and I sat on the couch watching an old movie we'd seen a dozen times, I brought it up. "Maybe it's time," I said softly. "Time to think about slowing down. For real this time."

He didn't respond right away. He just stared at the screen, his jaw tight. "I'm not ready to feel useless," he finally said. "I still have something to give."

"You do," I told him. "You always will. But maybe it's time to give in a different way."

We didn't finish the movie that night. Instead, we talked, really talked about fears, purpose, finances, and pride. About what it meant to step back without stepping away. About legacy, and how maybe the bravest thing wasn't holding on, but letting go with dignity.

It wasn't a decision made overnight, but the shift had already begun. The kind you feel in your bones before your mind can fully catch up. And for the first time in a long while, we were preparing for what came next together.

After much encouragement from friends and family, Guillermo finally submitted his retirement paperwork. The school was heartbroken to see him go. On his last day, the principal, staff and students showered him with gifts and handwritten cards. A large banner stretched across the auditorium, reading *Thank You, Mr. Martinez.*

He stood before the students and spoke from the heart, wishing them well and reminding them to stay out of trouble. A few brave students stepped up to read aloud letters they had written to him, some funny, some heartfelt, all unforgettable. Carolina and I sat in the front row, tears streaming down our faces, overwhelmed by the love and legacy he was leaving behind.

Guillermo walked out of the school for the last time, his head held high, grateful, humbled, and proud of the lives he had touched. He walked with a cane now, his body tired, and the effects of his MS becoming harder to ignore, but his spirit remained steady. Retirement wasn't an ending; it was a change. A new season, one where healing, rest, and rediscovery could finally take the lead.

***

At first, the days felt strange. Guillermo no longer woke up to the sound of an alarm or the hum of morning routines. The house was quieter, slower. He tried to fill the time reading, tinkering with the airplane models Antonio had sent him, or watching old documentaries, though some mornings, I'd find him at the window, quiet and far away." Some days, he had physical therapy.

There were good days, when his energy returned and we'd take walks through the neighborhood, hand in hand like we used to. There were hard days too, when the fatigue hit him like a wave and his legs refused to cooperate. He would get angry and frustrated. He hated feeling dependent, even though I never minded helping. That was the part no one warned us about—how much mourning could live inside change, even when you know it's for the best.

I officially accepted my promotion offer at work. After years of showing up early, staying late, and going above and beyond, someone finally noticed. I was proud, of course, but the timing felt complicated. While I was stepping into something new, Guillermo was stepping away. Our paths, once parallel, were now headed in different directions. I worried it would create distance between us. Instead, it brought us closer.

We found a new routine—me coming home from work to find him in the kitchen trying a new recipe, or him walking me to my car in the mornings with his coffee in hand. He was adjusting to a new identity, just as I was stepping into mine. And somehow, through it all, we were still learning ourselves at this stage of our lives.

Chapter 18

The holidays came faster than we expected. Carolina had plans to visit, and Antonio said he had a surprise in store. Karime offered to take her father to his follow-up appointment. It would be our first Christmas with Guillermo retired, and everything about it felt different, like life had other plans, plans to let us spend time together.

Guillermo had officially been retired for a few weeks, and while the dynamics of our home had changed, the spirit inside it had not. The tree was up by the first week of December thanks to Carolina, who insisted on helping me decorate it, even though she complained about the old ornaments I refused to throw away.

"This angel has no wings, Mami," she teased, holding up the same tinsel-wrapped figurine we'd used since our first apartment.

"She's been through a lot," I replied. "Like all of us."

Guillermo sat on the couch watching us, a blanket over his lap and a coy smile on his face. While his health was declining, he still offered his opinion and corrected us when we skipped a step in the tradition.

Karime came home the weekend before Christmas and offered to take her father to his follow-up appointment. She'd been asking more questions lately about his condition, his symptoms, and what the doctors were saying. She had grown into a caretaker before any of us had the language for it.

"I can take him, Mami. I don't mind."

He didn't argue. Maybe he was getting used to being cared for. Or maybe, he just liked riding with his daughter, letting her fuss over him while pretending he didn't like it.

Meanwhile, Antonio had been awfully quiet in our family group chat, responding only with vague one-word texts. Carolina and I were convinced he was hiding something.

"He better not be bringing a stray puppy or a roommate who has nowhere else to go," Carolina joked.

"He better not be bringing a secret wife," I countered.

The truth turned out to be even more surprising.

When Antonio pulled into the driveway three days before Christmas, he wasn't alone. From the passenger side, a beautiful, petite woman with a copper-toned complexion and shoulder-length hair stepped out. She wore a soft wool coat, a noticeable baby bump, and a warm, graceful smile. Antonio walked around to her side, placed a hand gently at the small of her back, and looked up at us on the porch like he was bracing for a wave of questions.

"Mami…this is Lisa," he said. "And we're having a baby."

I opened my mouth, but no words came out—just a loud, startled scream. I probably scared the poor girl. Guillermo rushed in with his cane from the other room, yelling, "*¿Qué pasó?*"

Lisa took a nervous step back, her hand instinctively resting on her belly. Her eyes were wide, unsure of whether to smile or brace herself. Antonio reached for her hand and gave her a reassuring squeeze, but I could see the tension in his jaw. He was trying to stay calm, but he was bracing for impact, too.

I stood there, stunned. My baby, Antonio, my only son, was going to be a father. I didn't ask if they were married or if they had plans to walk down the aisle. None of that mattered in that moment. All I knew was that Guillermo and I were about to become grandparents. And somehow, in the midst of shock and emotion, excitement began to rise in my chest like an inflated balloon I couldn't hold down.

Guillermo looked between the two of them, then at me. "*¿Qué es esto?*" he asked, still catching his breath.

Antonio stood tall, trying to sound confident. "Papi… We're having a baby."

Guillermo's eyes twitched with something I couldn't quite place. Shock, yes, but also a deep, searching concern. He walked over slowly, placing a steadying hand on the back of the nearest chair. Then, after a long pause, he looked at Lisa and said softly, "*Bienvenida, mija.*"

Lisa's eyes welled with relief. "Thank you, sir."

Guillermo nodded and offered a small, tired smile. "Call me Guillermo. Or better yet, *abuelo*. Since that's what I'll be now."

The tension broke, just a little. We all laughed awkward, teary and unsure, but it was a start.

Later that night, after everyone had settled in and the house was finally quiet, I found Lisa in the kitchen putting away a few dishes.

"Can't sleep?" I asked, pouring myself a glass of water.

She shook her head. "Too many thoughts."

I nodded. "That makes two of us."

She hesitated before speaking again. "I hope I didn't mess everything up. I know this isn't how families usually share news like this."

I walked over and placed a hand gently on her arm. "Families don't come with instructions. And if they did, ours would've tossed the manual a long time ago."

Lisa smiled, her eyes glossy. "I just want to do right by him. By all of you."

"You already are," I said. "You're here. You're carrying his child. That means something. And now, you're part of this family, whether you are ready or not."

She let out a sigh, the kind that sounded like a release.

"We're not perfect," I added, "but we're full of love. And that baby? That baby is already surrounded by it."

After everyone went to bed, I found Guillermo in our bedroom, sitting on the edge of the bed with his cane leaning against the nightstand. The lamp was still on, casting a soft glow across his face. He looked up when I came in, but didn't say anything right away.

I sat beside him, waiting.

"Well," I finally said, "our son is having a baby."

Guillermo exhaled, long and slow. "I wasn't ready to hear that tonight."

"Neither was I," I admitted, "but here we are."

He nodded, still staring ahead. "She seems sweet. Nervous, but sweet."

"She is," I said. "And she's carrying our grandchild."

He rubbed the back of his neck like he was trying to massage the weight of the day away. "Do you think he's ready?"

I smiled gently. "Were we?"

Guillermo chuckled at that. "Fair enough."

"I saw the way he looked at her, Guillermo. He's scared, but he's showing up. That counts for something."

"Should we ask him if he's planning to marry her? I don't want to pressure them, but still… When we found out we were pregnant, I offered you my hand in marriage. It just felt like the right thing to do, the responsible thing to do." Guillermo leaned back against the headboard and looked at me for the first time that night. "How do you feel?"

I thought about it for a second, then said, "Like something new is beginning. I'm still catching up to it, but deep down…I'm happy. It feels like life is reminding us it's still moving forward, no matter what stage we're in."

Guillermo reached for my hand and gave it a soft squeeze. "I guess it's our turn to show them how to build a family."

I rested my head on his shoulder. "We already have."

We sat like that for a while, listening to the house settle around us, the heater humming, the wind brushing against the windows. In a world that never stopped changing, this moment felt still. And sacred.

"Tomorrow, let's talk to Antonio about his future plans, about support, about what the future might look like. Tonight, we let ourselves simply be grateful for our grandbaby."

****

Carolina's high school reunion was scheduled for the Friday before Christmas. She debated whether to go, unsure if it would be worth it. After helping decorate the house and seeing her father in better spirits, she finally said, "Why not?"

She wore a burgundy wrap dress, and soft curls framed her face just right. As she stood in front of the mirror adjusting her earrings, she looked both nervous and radiant.

"You look beautiful, *mija*," I told her. "Just go, have fun. You don't have to stay long."

"I know," she said, picking up her purse.

I didn't press. Sometimes, mothers know when to ask questions and when to simply go with the flow.

She got home around midnight, cheeks flushed from the cold. She came into the kitchen while I was wrapping presents and poured herself a glass of wine.

"You stayed late," I said.

She nodded. "It was actually…really nice. I saw a few old friends, and one I didn't expect."

I looked up, curious. "Someone special?"

She smiled shyly, like the version of her I hadn't seen since college. "Jared. Remember him? He was a year ahead of me. Played trumpet in the jazz band."

"Yes, I remember him. Nice looking guy with dimples."

Carolina laughed. "That's the one."

She didn't say more, and I didn't press, but when she walked out of the kitchen humming a tune I didn't recognize, I knew something in her had changed.

Christmas arrived with the kind of magic only grown children can bring. No one woke up at dawn, but when the coffee started brewing and the smell of cinnamon filled the air, one by one they emerged, Karime in her robe, Carolina in fuzzy socks, and Antonio slipping out of the guest room, hand in hand with Lisa.

We gathered in the living room, opening gifts and sipping café con leche. Soon, wrapping paper covered the floor like confetti, curling ribbons trailing off in every direction. Everyone sat around the tree, tearing into presents with the excitement of children, never mind that we were all grown.

Antonio handed out his gifts to his sisters, Carolina letting out a dramatic screech when she opened hers. "Thank you, Brother! I love this sweater dress. Did you actually pick this out yourself?" She held up a soft cream knit with gold threading along the sleeves, stylish and just her taste.

Before Antonio could respond, Lisa grinned knowingly from the couch.

Karime raised an eyebrow, amused. "Okay, okay, Antonio. You've clearly stepped your gift game up this year."

He shrugged, trying to play it cool. "I've been paying attention."

We laughed, and for a moment, time folded in on itself, just family, just joy, just love.

Then Karime handed a small, neatly wrapped box to Guillermo.

"For you, Papi," she said, placing it gently in his lap.

Guillermo looked surprised. "What's this?"

"Just open it."

Inside was a custom leather-bound journal with gold lettering that read: "For the Next Chapter – *Con Amor, Tu Familia.*" Tucked inside the first page was a handwritten note: *Write it all down. Your stories, your thoughts, your memories. We want to remember everything.*

Guillermo blinked fast, then cleared his throat. "*Gracias, mi amor*," he said, his voice barely above a whisper.

He looked at me, and I knew he was holding back tears.

Carolina handed me an envelope next. "This one's for you, Mami."

Inside was a gift certificate for a weekend spa retreat with massages, facials, the works.

"You've been taking care of everyone else for so long," she said. "Time to take care of you."

I put a hand over my heart. "You kids are going to make me cry."

"That's kind of the point," Karime teased.

And just like that, Christmas wasn't about the gifts at all; it was about how seen we felt, how loved. Every package, every laugh, every tear was a reminder of everything we'd built and everything still to come.

Guillermo sat in his favorite chair, a knit blanket over his knees, watching us with soft eyes.

At one point, Lisa handed him a small wrapped box. "This is from me…and the baby," she said.

Guillermo opened it slowly. Inside was a wooden picture frame with a sonogram photo and the words *Abuelo, coming soon.*

He stared at it for a long moment before lifting his glasses to wipe his eyes.

"Well," he said, voice cracking. "Looks like I've got a new job after all."

We laughed, and cried, and for a moment, nothing else mattered.

****

Dinner was loud, joyful, and just a little chaotic, exactly how it should be. The air was thick with the scent of garlic and onions simmering in sofrito, the sweetness of caramelized plantains, and the warm, earthy aroma of black beans stewing with bay leaves. Roasted pork filled the room with its savory, citrusy fragrance, and every time someone opened the oven, a wave of spices, cumin, oregano, and a hint of smoke floated through the house like a promise. It smelled like home. Like history. Like love served on a plate.

Carolina made arroz amarillo y pollo guisado, Karime prepared a salad with citrus vinaigrette she learned in Cambridge, and Antonio helped Lisa stay off her feet while sneaking second helpings of lechon asado. I cooked the black beans, white rice, yuca and platano maduro. The table was full not just of food, but of laughter, teasing, and stories we hadn't told in years.

At one point, Guillermo raised his glass. "To family," he said, his voice steady but emotional. "To new beginnings…and to letting go of what no longer serves us."

We clinked glasses and sat in the glow of it all—candlelight flickering against wine glasses, the hum of Jackson Five Christmas music playing in the background, and the miracle of being together.

Later that night, after the dishes were done and everyone had gone to bed or curled up on couches with blankets, Guillermo and I sat alone on the back porch. The air was cold, but we didn't mind. He had a scarf wrapped around his neck, and my hands tucked into his lap.

"It was a good Christmas," he said.

"One of the best," I agreed.

He looked out into the yard, where the lights we'd strung weeks ago still blinked gently against the fence. "I didn't think I'd feel...useful again," he admitted. "Watching everyone tonight reminded me that I still matter. Not because I am retired. Just because I'm here."

I leaned my head on his shoulder. "You've always mattered, but I'm glad you finally saw it, too."

We sat there for a long while in deep thought, the kind only love can make comfortable. And just like that, Christmas wasn't just a holiday. It was a homecoming we hadn't even realized we needed.

Chapter 19

"Navidades con la Sonora Matancera"

The next morning, the house slowly came to life with the smell of Café Bustelo, buttered toast, and the low hum of salsa on the kitchen radio. Carolina was already up, wrapped in a thick robe, flipping through a magazine at the table. Karime sat beside her, scrolling her phone with one hand and nursing a mug of tea with the other.

Antonio walked in last, rubbing sleep from his eyes, followed closely by Lisa, whose growing belly now seemed impossible to ignore. She gave us all a soft smile, one hand resting protectively across her front like a reflex she'd developed overnight.

"Buenos días," I said, handing her a plate.

"Gracias," she replied, her voice quiet but warm.

Guillermo sat at the head of the table, cane resting beside his chair, looking more rested than I'd seen him in days. His eyes moved from face to face, like he was taking inventory of his blessings.

"Antonio," he said between bites, "did you ever think you'd be up before noon while visiting home?"

Antonio smirked. "I've got new responsibilities now, old man."

Everyone laughed.

Carolina raised her brow. "So, are we going to talk about the baby or pretend y'all didn't just drop a bomb in the living room last night?"

Karime chimed in. "Seriously, I want to know everything. How far along? When's the due date?

Lisa looked overwhelmed for a second, but Antonio placed his hand gently over hers.

"We're about five months," he said. "Due in April."

"April," I repeated. "Christmas in April."

Guillermo and I exchanged a glance, both of us feeling the weight of that sentence, how symbolic it was. Our child, having a child in the month that changed our lives so many years ago.

Lisa spoke softly. "I know it's not what anyone expected, but I'm committed to making this work with Antonio, with all of you."

"You're here," I said. "That's a good start."

The conversation drifted into baby names and nursery colors. Antonio joked about naming the baby "Guillermito" if it were a boy, to which Guillermo rolled his eyes and muttered, *"Dios nos libre."* Laughter filled the kitchen again.

But I noticed Karime had grown quiet. She pushed her eggs around her plate, only half-listening. Something was on her mind.

After breakfast, she found me in the laundry room folding towels. "Mami, can I talk to you for a second?"

"Of course, *mija*." I turned toward her, already sensing the shift in her energy.

She leaned against the dryer, arms crossed. "About Papi's appointment…"

I stopped folding. "He didn't say much when you got back," I said gently. "Should I be worried?"

Karime hesitated, biting her bottom lip the way she did as a little girl when she had something difficult to say. "The doctor was kind, but direct. Papi's MS is progressing. Not aggressively, but enough that they're adjusting his medication. There's more nerve damage in his legs than before, and they're concerned about his balance. That fall wasn't just a fluke."

My chest tightened. Karime held my hand. "How did your father react to what the doctor was saying?"

"He didn't say much, just listened. The doctor said the fatigue alone could be dangerous if he pushes himself too much."

I nodded slowly, trying to keep my face composed. "Did he seem upset?"

"He acted like it didn't bother him, but I saw it, Mami. I saw how hard he was trying to hold it together. He hates feeling like this."

I sat on the edge of the laundry basket and exhaled. "He's always been the one carrying us. Even when he was tired. Even when we didn't know."

Karime walked over and placed a hand on my shoulder. "Maybe now it's our turn to carry him."

I looked up at her, my daughter, now a woman, now someone I could lean on and felt both sadness and pride rise in my chest. "We'll figure it out," I said softly. "Together."

She nodded, and for a moment, we stood in that small room, surrounded by fresh laundry and the realization that life was twisting and turning again.

That night, after everyone had gone to bed, I found Guillermo in the den watching an old Western with the volume turned low. He looked relaxed, but his eyes gave him away. Distant, tired in a way that went beyond the body.

I sat down next to him on the couch, curling my feet beneath me.

"How are you feeling?" I asked, keeping my voice soft.

He shrugged, eyes still on the screen. "Fine."

I waited a moment before speaking again. "Karime told me about the appointment."

His jaw clenched slightly, then relaxed. "Of course she did."

"She was worried," I said. "And so am I."

He finally turned to look at me, his expression unreadable. "There's nothing to worry about. It's just…part of it. I've been managing this for years."

"I know," I said. "But you don't have to manage it alone."

He looked away again, the glow from the TV flickering across his face. "I just don't want to feel like a burden."

"You're not," I said, without hesitation. "You never have been."

"I'm used to being the one people depend on, not the one needing help getting off the damn couch."

I reached for his hand, taking hold and weaving his fingers through mine. "You've been strong for us for so long. Let us show up for you now… That's not weakness, Guillermo. That's trust. That's love."

He closed his eyes for a beat. "I'm scared," he said finally. "Not of the illness. Of what it might take from me. From us."

I moved closer and pressed my cheek against his. "It won't take us. You hear me? We're in this together."

He nodded slowly, and his hand squeezed mine.

"Okay," he whispered. "Okay."

A moment later, Antonio walked in and sat down beside his father. There was a brief silence before Guillermo spoke. "Are there any plans to get married?" Guillermo looked at him, eyebrows raised but calm.

Antonio rubbed the back of his neck. "We're not ready yet. The pregnancy was a surprise that neither of us was expecting. I'm committed, though. To her, and to the baby."

"Have you moved in together?" Guillermo asked.

"Yeah. Just recently."

"What took so long?"

Antonio smiled a little. "Lisa likes her own space. Took me a while to convince her we needed to build a home together, not just a relationship."

Guillermo nodded, thoughtful. "That's fair. Just make sure you keep showing up—for her, for the baby, and for yourself."

"I will," Antonio said. "Every day."

Guillermo leaned back, his cane resting by the side of the chair. His gaze drifted to the framed photo of our family on the bookshelf, the one taken when the kids were little, all missing teeth and holiday sweaters.

"You know," he began, "when your mother and I found out we were expecting Karime, I didn't have a clue what I was doing. I was scared out of my mind. We didn't have much money, just a two-bedroom apartment, and I was still trying to finish school."

I smiled quietly, remembering. "We were barely more than kids ourselves."

Guillermo chuckled. "I thought the 'man thing to do' was to figure it all out on my own. Provide, fix, solve. I learned real quick that being a man wasn't about knowing everything. It was about showing up. Being present. Growing up alongside your family."

He turned back to Antonio, his expression more serious now. "You've already taken the first step, Son. Just don't stop there. You don't have to be perfect. Just be there with your whole heart. That's what lasts."

Antonio nodded, his voice steady. "Thank you, Papi. That means a lot."

Guillermo looked at him for a long moment, then smiled. "Besides, you've got us. You're not in this alone."

Just then, Lisa appeared in the doorway, rubbing her belly. "Is everything okay in here?"

"All good," Antonio said, getting up to meet her halfway.

Guillermo and I shared a glance as we watched them together, unsure, figuring it out, and slowly becoming a family. Just like we once did.

Later that afternoon, Karime and I stood side by side in the laundry room, folding towels. I said, "Lisa seems really kind and thoughtful. You can tell she's going to be a great mom, even if this wasn't part of the plan."

Karime was quiet for a moment. "Neither was Papi's retirement. Nor was his MS getting worse. Or any of this, really."

"No," I said. "But life has a way of making room for the unexpected. It forces you sometimes to confront things head-on."

She looked at me, folding slowly. "Were you scared? When you found out you were pregnant with me?"

I gave a soft laugh. "Terrified. But also…determined. Your father and I didn't have much, but we had love, and that love taught us how to keep going. One day, one decision at a time."

Karime nodded, eyes low. "Sometimes I wonder if I'll ever have that."

"You will, baby," I said gently. "It may not look exactly the way you imagined. It almost never does. Just keep leading with love. The rest follows."

She smiled, and for a moment, I saw the little girl who used to sit on the dryer, swinging her legs while I folded these same towels. Now, she stood beside me, grown, steady, and strong.

We kept folding in silence, the hum of the dryer the only sound between us, but it wasn't empty. It was full of understanding, of lineage, of the invisible thread connecting generations of women who knew how to make something whole out of whatever life handed them.

****

As everyone was gathering their suitcases and preparing to leave, Carolina paused at the door and said, "Wait. When was the last time we took a family portrait?"

I laughed. "Let's just say you were knee-high with two missing teeth, and I had not one strand of gray hair."

"We're all here," she said. "Let's take one."

"Okay, everyone, get in position," Karime called out, taking charge.

We all shuffled over to the tree, arranging ourselves into a loose, familiar pose. Guillermo stood proudly in front, wearing the reindeer sweater I bought him, his cane resting at his side like a badge of honor.

"On the count of three!" Karime said.

Antonio started jogging in place, making us all laugh.

"One... two... three—" The Polaroid camera snapped three times, capturing blurry movement, wide smiles, and a moment we'd never forget.

After the house had emptied out and the calmness had settled in, I curled up on the couch with a cup of tea and opened my book.. There it was, the photo. Blurry around the edges, a little crooked, and absolutely perfect.

Carolina was mid-laugh, her hand resting on Karime's shoulder. Antonio stood behind Lisa, one arm protectively around her, the other frozen mid-air like he was still jogging in place. Guillermo stood tall, smiling. Not the forced kind, but the soft one he gave when he was truly at peace. And me, tucked right in the center, surrounded by everything we had built.

I stared at it for a long time, then found a frame and placed the picture in it and placed it on the end table in the living room, where the pictures stay.

A reminder that even with all the unexpected twists and aches, this was the life I prayed for. Imperfect. Evolving. Full. And beautifully ours.

Chapter 20

"Gracias"

The decorations came down slowly that year. Not because we forgot, but because none of us were in a rush to let go of the feeling that had settled over the house. The kind of stillness that only follows after laughter and full hearts.

By New Year's, Carolina was back in New York City, Antonio and Lisa had returned to their townhouse in Washington, DC, and Karime stayed around a few extra days, helping with errands and keeping an eye on her father before heading off to Miami.

The house had settled back into its usual routine, just Guillermo and me, only this time, it didn't feel empty. It felt like something new had taken root. I couldn't quite name it, but I welcomed it.

We had so much to be grateful for. We were going to be grandparents. I never imagined I'd live to see this moment, and now that it was here, I could hardly contain my joy.

One morning, just as I was preparing for work and Guillermo was in the shower, the phone rang.

"It's Antonio," came the voice on the other end—breathless, nervous, and full of adrenaline. "We're at the hospital. Lisa's in labor."

When Guillermo came out of the bathroom, I shared the news with a trembling smile. Not long after that call, Lisa gave birth to a baby girl. Six pounds, eight ounces. We were officially grandparents.

Guillermo and I cried right there on the phone with Antonio. We could barely get the words out, overwhelmed with emotion.

Not long after, the next call came. "Mom, when are you and Dad coming down to help out with the baby?" And just like that, a new chapter had begun.

A few days later, Guillermo and I packed our bags and boarded an early morning flight, bleary-eyed but buzzing with anticipation. He wore his nicest sweater and carried his cane with pride, walking a little slower these days, but every step was filled with purpose.

When we arrived at the hospital, Antonio met us in the lobby. His eyes were tired but soft with wonder, the look of a man who had just stepped into something bigger than himself.

"She's perfect," he said, hugging us both. "Lisa's resting, but she's doing great. They are keeping our baby girl a little longer for observation to monitor her mild jaundice. Come on, I want you to meet your granddaughter."

We followed him down a hallway, and when we entered the room, time seemed to pause. Lisa smiled from the hospital bed, pale but glowing. She looked up and motioned to the bassinet beside her.

"Here she is," she said.

Guillermo and I walked over slowly. I don't know what I expected, but the moment I saw her tiny, warm, swaddled in pink with a full head of dark hair, I felt my knees soften.

"Oh, Guillermo," I whispered.

He didn't say anything at first, just leaned in close. I watched his face change as he looked at her. The lines of worry and age seemed to melt for a moment, replaced by something lighter. He reached out and touched her little hand.

"*Hola, mi nieta,*" he said, voice low and trembling. "*Soy tu abuelito.*"

Lisa gently picked up the baby and placed her in Guillermo's arms. He held her like something sacred, his hands steady despite the tremors he sometimes tried to hide. Tears filled his eyes, and for a while, none of us spoke.

Then it was my turn.

Lisa handed her to me, and I cradled her against my chest, swaying slightly like I had done with all three of my children. She smelled like baby powder and something else—something brand new. I couldn't wait to dab *Agua de Violetas*, baby cologne.

"She's so small," I murmured.

"But she makes everything feel big," Guillermo added, still standing beside me, his arm resting on my back.

That night, as we sat together in the dim hospital room, Guillermo and I held hands and watched Antonio rock his daughter gently in the corner. Lisa drifted in and out of sleep and hallway chatter, the soundtrack to her new life beginning.

A few days later, Lisa and the baby were discharged, and we followed them home to their townhouse, a cozy four-bedroom with baby supplies tucked into every corner. There were diapers stacked by the couch, a bassinet in the living room, and a baby monitor blinking softly near the bedroom door.

Lisa looked exhausted, but she was trying, swaddling the baby with care, reading every label twice, setting alarms on her phone for feedings.

"*Mija,*" I said gently, "you don't have to do everything perfectly. Just be present. She needs your love more than your checklist."

Lisa exhaled, letting her shoulders drop. "I just want to get it right."

"You will," I said, cupping her cheek. "And we're here. You're not alone."

That afternoon, Guillermo sat in the rocker by the window, humming an old *bolero* as he held the baby to his chest. Antonio stood nearby, watching them with a mix of pride and disbelief.

"I still can't believe I'm someone's father," he said, shaking his head with a quiet laugh.

"Get used to it," Guillermo replied, without looking up. "It only gets better."

Meanwhile, I moved through the kitchen, prepping ropa vieja, white rice, tostones, and a pot of black beans. The scents of garlic and tomato sauce filled the space, bringing a little warmth and savory to their new way of living.

I sat with Lisa while she nursed the baby, coaching her through the discomfort and the miracle of it. "Everything changes," I whispered. "But not all at once. You'll find your way."

She looked at me with tired eyes and nodded. "Thank you. For being here. For everything."

I smiled and brushed a curl from her forehead. "This is what family does."

A few months later, we returned for a small blessing ceremony. Just a close family, a few candles, and one tiny white dress that had belonged to Karime. We took photos in the park, the baby wrapped in a crocheted blanket, Guillermo in his reindeer sweater again, because now it was "lucky."

As I watched Antonio rock his daughter under a blooming magnolia tree, I felt the same ache and joy I had when I first held him. It was like repeating itself, but gentler and wiser. And this time, we had front-row seats.

Just weeks after the birth of their daughter, Antonio received his deployment orders. He didn't want to go. That much was clear in the way he held Rosa Alicia a little tighter each night, in the way he looked at Lisa when he thought no one was watching. But duty called, and like so many before him, he went.

I remember the day he left. It was overcast, and the air felt unusually still, like the sky itself was holding its breath. We stood on the front porch, watching him place his duffel bag in the trunk. Guillermo put a hand on his shoulder, firm, proud, but trembling slightly.

"Come back to us," he said.

"I will," Antonio replied, his voice low, his jaw clenched.

He kissed Lisa softly, whispered something in her ear, then leaned down to brush his lips across the forehead of his newborn daughter. She yawned and curled her tiny fingers around his pinky, as if she knew. And then he was gone.

We didn't hear from him for four months. At first, we told ourselves no news is good news. Maybe he was in a remote region. Maybe communication was limited. Maybe he was just focused, staying safe, keeping his head down. But deep down, I knew. A mother always knows.

The knock came on a rainy Thursday afternoon. I was folding baby clothes in the living room when Lisa answered the door. I heard her gasp before I saw the color drain from her face.

When she finally looked at me, her lips parted, but no sound came out.

Guillermo stood by the door, listening while the officers delivered the news that shattered our world: Antonio had been killed by enemy fire. I dropped to my knees and screamed. I couldn't believe what I was hearing; my only son was dead.

He died during a nighttime raid and ambush, they said. Quick, they said. As if that would somehow ease the pain from our loss.

But nothing could. Not the carefully chosen words, not the folded flag they would soon place in our hands, not the way people lowered their voices when they spoke his name.

My son was dead, and in his place, he left a daughter who would never remember the sound of his voice.

Guillermo and I were numb. It felt like a movie looping in my mind, playing the same devastating scene again and again. We fought back tears, trying to be strong for our daughters. We waited until nightfall to call them. I couldn't bring myself to do it any sooner. Guillermo sat beside me on the edge of our bed, the phone in one hand and the other pressed against his temple as if he needed it to hold himself together.

We called Carolina first. She answered on the third ring, cheerful as always. "Hey, Mami! I was just about to call you. I saw the cutest baby boots today."

I had to interrupt. My voice cracked before I got the words out.

"Carolina… *Mija*… There's something we need to tell you."

Her tone shifted instantly. "What's happened?"

I looked at Guillermo. He nodded, and I spoke the words we'd been carrying like stones in our backs.

"It's Antonio. He was killed."

There was silence on the other end of the line. Then a sharp inhale.

"No…" she screamed. "No. No, no, no."

Her cries broke through the phone like glass shattering, and all I could do was hold the phone close and whisper, "I'm so sorry. I'm so sorry."

We called Karime next. Guillermo tried to speak, but the words caught in his throat. So I did it again.

She didn't cry right away. She didn't say anything for a long time.

"Antonio?" she finally asked, as if she hadn't heard me right. "Our Antonio?"

"Yes, *mi amor*."

I could hear her breathing hard, trying to keep it together. "I spoke to him a few months ago," she said sadly. "He called me before he left. Said he'd be home in time for Rosa Alicia's first birthday."

I closed my eyes. "I know, baby. I know."

That night, all four of us cried in separate cities, holding onto a pain too big for words. But in that grief, we were still tethered. Still a family broken, but unbroken.

The next day, they both came home. Carolina walked in with red eyes and arms full of food, because that's what she does when she doesn't know what else to do. Karime came with a framed photo of the three of them as kids, already setting it by the crib.

We didn't have to say much. We just held each other. And in that moment, we began the long journey of remembering him together.

In the weeks that followed, we rallied around Lisa. Guillermo built a wooden cradle by hand, something to keep his hands busy, something that felt like purpose. I cooked, cleaned, and rocked the baby to sleep when Lisa couldn't bring herself to move.

Rosa Alicia, too young to understand, became our light. Her tiny milestones, smiling, holding her head up, gripping our fingers, became small victories. A way for us to hold on.

She was proof that Antonio had been here. That he had lived. That he had loved and through her, we would carry him forward.

The funeral was held on a gray, somber morning, the sky mirroring our grief. The church was packed with family, friends, and fellow soldiers. Even old neighbors who hadn't seen Antonio in years came to pay their respects.

Lisa sat in the front pew, her face pale, a tissue clenched tightly in her hand. Baby Rosa Alicia was cradled in her arms, wrapped in a soft white blanket with tiny yellow ducks on the edges, one of the last things Antonio had picked out before he left.

I sat beside Guillermo, holding his hand as the chaplain spoke. The words blurred together, phrases like "honor," "sacrifice," and "service" echoed throughout the cathedral. None of them could fully know our son the way we did. Not the boy who made up raps in his bedroom. Not the man who swore he'd be a better father than he ever knew. Not the new dad who cried the first time he held his daughter in his arms.

Yasmine held Carolina and Karime close, their shoulders trembling beneath her arms. Pedro, Elba, Alberto, Isabelle, Maya and Carmen sat quietly nearby. My supervisor and a few of my colleagues from the hospital came to show their support, their presence comforting. Several teachers and staff members from Guillermo's school filled the pew behind us, their heads bowed in respect.

The folded flag was presented to Lisa by a young officer with solemn eyes. She accepted it with both hands, her face a picture of strength and devastation.

When we returned home, the women from the church had organized a repast in our living room. The house filled with the comforting aroma of homemade food, baked macaroni and cheese, roasted chicken, rice and beans. Guests sat on couches and folding chairs, balancing paper plates on their laps, drinks resting on the floor beside them.

Everyone shared memories of Antonio. His basketball coach spoke first, his voice thick with emotion, recalling Antonio's discipline and how he led the team by example. Former teammates followed, each one offering stories about his determination, his loyalty, and the way he always lifted others up, even in the heat of the game.

As the sun began to dip and the plates emptied, the room settled into a heavy calm. The kind that comes after a storm, still thick with emotion but softened by shared memory.

I stood in the doorway, watching everyone. Lisa sat in the corner rocking Rosa Alicia, her eyes distant but focused, as if holding the baby was the only thing keeping her grounded. Karime helped clear plates, while Carolina refilled drinks and passed out napkins. Yasmine was folding blankets that had been draped across chairs.

This was grief, I realized, not just sorrow, but care in motion, people doing small things to hold each other up.

I stepped outside for a moment, needing air. The sky was painted in fading shades of pink and orange. I looked up and whispered, "Antonio I hope you see all this. I hope you know how loved you are."

Guillermo stepped outside and stood beside me. He didn't say anything at first, just took my hand and looked out at the yard, where a few guests remained, engaged in conversation.

"I want to say something to our guests," he said. "Before everyone leaves."

"*Sigue*, Guillermo." We stepped back inside, and Guillermo walked slowly, steadying himself with his cane. The room grew quiet as he began to speak, and all conversations came to a complete stop.

"Thank you all for being here," he began, his voice soft but steady. "For loving our son. For standing with us."

He looked around the room at Lisa, at the baby, at the familiar faces of friends and neighbors, each one holding their own memories of Antonio

"Antonio was many things. A son, a brother, a teammate…a soldier. What I'm most proud of is the man he became. He gave his all to his family, to his country, and to his daughter. He left us too soon, but he left us with a piece of himself in her." He looked toward Rosa Alicia, asleep now in Lisa's arms. "So we're going to keep showing up. For her and for each other. Just like he would have wanted us to."

There were soft sounds of someone weeping, and a few nods from those who understood his pain. Guillermo slowly sat down, and I placed my hand over his, recognizing that we had buried a piece of ourselves that day, but we were still here with laughter and tears spreading throughout the room, for the boy we raised and the man we lost.

Later that evening, after everyone had gone, what remained were the soft sounds of Lisa rocking the baby at night, and Guillermo walking through the house like he had forgotten why he entered each room. I tried to be strong for everyone, but grief has a way of finding those little cracks.

One night, after Lisa had gone to bed and Guillermo was asleep, I stood in Rosa Alicia's nursery. She was dozing in her crib, her little chest rising and falling in rhythm. I placed my hand on her back and whispered, "Your daddy loved you. He wanted to be here. He should be here," and the tears wouldn't stop falling.

Everyone went back to their normal routine. Lisa returned to work at the Pentagon, and Carolina went back to her life in NYC.

Karime soon moved back up north so that she could be closer to us. She found a condo a few towns over and began working as an ER doctor for the largest hospital in New Jersey. Guillermo and I were so proud of Karime.

****

Depression hit me like a ton of bricks. I couldn't leave my bed for what seemed like months. My doctor told me that I was on the brink of a nervous breakdown. Guillermo tried everything he could to help ease the pain, but nothing worked. I no longer wanted to deal with life. My son had been killed. How was I supposed to function without him?

Some days, I didn't speak. I barely ate. The walls of our home felt like they were caving in, filled with the sounds of Antonio's laughter, his footsteps, his music. I'd find myself standing in the hallway outside his room, hand on the doorknob, unable to go in. Just standing there, aching.

But healing doesn't arrive all at once. It tiptoes in small and stubborn,

One morning, Karime brought me a cup of tea and sat beside me on the edge of the bed. She didn't say much. She just held my hand, her thumb gently rubbing over mine, the way I used to do for her when she had nightmares as a child. Something about that moment cracked something open in me. Not enough to stand, not yet—but enough to breathe a little deeper.

Another day, Carolina left a book on my nightstand. "When you're ready," she said. It sat there untouched for weeks. Then one day, I picked it up. Read a page. Then another.

Guillermo began reading the Bible to me in the evenings. Not with the expectation that I'd respond—just so I could hear the sound of someone believing in me when I couldn't. Grief didn't leave, but over time, it stopped being the only voice in the room.

One Sunday morning, months after Antonio's funeral, I got dressed for church. It wasn't anything dramatic, no big decision, no burst of energy. I just woke up, walked to my closet, and picked out a dress I hadn't worn in ages. Guillermo looked surprised when he saw me buttoning my dress, but he didn't say a word. He just smiled, got his coat, and walked with me to the car.

The sanctuary was already half full when we arrived. Familiar faces turned toward us, some with warm smiles, others with eyes that held the same sorrow mine did. Nobody asked questions. They didn't need to. They just scooted over and made room on the pew.

When the choir began singing, "Blessed Assurance," I felt something shift in my chest. The lump in my throat rose fast and hot, but I didn't run. I let the tears fall, and for the first time in a long while, I wasn't ashamed of how I was feeling.

After service, an older woman I barely knew hugged me tight and whispered, "I've been praying for your strength." It unraveled me and stitched me up all at once.

I went home and cooked dinner. Nothing fancy—just rice, beans, and a baked chicken. It was the first meal I'd made in months. I called Karime and Carolina and told them to come by. When they walked through the door and smelled the food, I saw the relief in their eyes.

We sat around the table, talking, laughing, and holding space for Antonio. No one said his name, but he was everywhere in the love that hadn't gone anywhere.

I was still grieving for my son. I would always grieve. But this time I was living again, one breath, one step, one small act of courage at a time.

****

Guillermo was out on the back porch, his Bible in his lap, but his eyes weren't reading. They were just watching the trees sway.

I stepped out and sat beside him. For a while, we didn't speak. The breeze carried the faint scent of lilacs from the neighbor's yard. Birds chirped like nothing in the world had changed.

"You're up," he said gently.

I nodded. "I think it's time."

He didn't ask what I meant. He just reached over and held my hand. "I've missed hearing your steps in the morning," he said. "Even the way you sigh when the coffee isn't hot enough."

I smiled faintly. "I wasn't sure I'd ever want to hear music again. Or smell food cooking. Or put lotion on my hands like it mattered. Then I saw her face this morning. Antonio's baby. His whole face is in hers."

Guillermo's voice cracked. "I know."

"She's here," I whispered, "and he's not. And that hurts, but I want her to grow up knowing joy, not just the shadow of what we lost." Guillermo nodded, squeezing my hand tighter.

The next day, I texted Lisa: Can we come visit?

She replied almost instantly: Please.

We drove down to Washington, DC. The closer we got, the more my hands shook, but Guillermo kept his hand on my knee the entire ride.

When we arrived, Lisa opened the door, holding Rosa Alicia in her arms. The baby's head was wrapped in a soft floral bonnet, her eyes curious, her cheeks full and warm like a ripe peach.

"Come in," Lisa said. "She's been fussy all morning. Maybe she knows something special's about to happen."

I stepped inside, and Guillermo followed. I knelt down on the couch and held out my arms.

"*Hola, mi amor*," I whispered. "It's your *abuela*."

Lisa placed her gently into my arms, and I sank into the cushions, cradling this little miracle against my chest. The baby stared at me for a long time, seriously, searching. Then, slowly, her tiny mouth curled into a half-smile.

It was like air returning to my lungs after months of shallow breathing.

"She looks just like Antonio," I murmured, brushing a finger over her forehead.

Lisa sat beside me. "Some days, I look at her, and it makes it worse. Some days, it makes it better. Today, it feels like both."

I nodded. "That's the truth of grief. It's not one feeling. It's a room full of them, and we learn to sit inside it."

She looked at me with tired, grateful eyes. "Thank you for coming."

"We'll always come," I said. "For you. For her. That's what family does."

Chapter 21

I returned to work feeling grateful, maybe even a little excited to settle back into my routine. Staying busy helped clear space in my mind, gave me something to focus on so I wouldn't spiral into thoughts of Antonio. Coming back wasn't easy. Everything felt different. A few times, I found myself hiding out in the employee's lounge, crying. The grief could be triggered by anything: a song on the radio, a patient's smile, the way someone said my name. But still, I held on. I pushed through. Because that's what I knew how to do.

One afternoon, after finishing rounds, I stopped by the break room to grab a cup of coffee. My hands were still shaking slightly—something about the way a young father had kissed his newborn's forehead had hit me hard. I didn't even realize I was holding my breath until the nurse beside me spoke.

"You okay, Rosa?"

It was Angela, one of the newer nurses. She was kind and didn't say much. We hadn't spoken much before.

I nodded quickly, too quickly. "Yeah, I'm fine. Just tired."

She didn't push. She just poured herself a cup of coffee and sat down beside me.

"You know," she said after a minute, "when my brother passed, I came back too soon. I thought keeping busy would make the pain go away."

I looked over at her, surprised. She didn't say it like she was offering advice, just the truth. "What helped you?"

She stared at her coffee for a moment. "Letting people see me. Letting them love me, even when I didn't feel like I deserved it."

I didn't say anything. But I nodded. And I sat with her a little longer than I normally would have because grief has a way of building walls around you, and sometimes healing looks like letting someone sit beside you, even when you're not ready to speak.

"I attend a group grief counseling session that meets once a week," she said. "If you're not doing anything, we meet for an hour on Wednesdays. It's during lunchtime, right here on the hospital campus, and it's free.

Every time I saw Angela after that, I found a way to avoid her. I didn't want to attend the group sessions partly because I'm a private person, and also because I didn't think sitting in a room full of strangers would help. It just didn't feel like a good use of my time.

But something stayed with me. The way Angela spoke so calmly, so confidently, like someone who had walked through the fire and came out with her skin still intact. I kept replaying her words, letting people love me, even when I didn't feel like I deserved it.

That Friday, I cried in the car before heading into work. No trigger, no warning, just an overwhelming wave that caught me off guard and didn't let up. I sat there, gripping the steering wheel, trying to breathe through it, and that's when I remembered the group.

The following Wednesday, I didn't tell anyone my plans. I just walked across campus during my lunch break and found the room

Angela had mentioned. It wasn't anything like I imagined. Just a circle of chairs, soft lighting, and a box of tissues in the center.

I sat in the back at first, near the door. I didn't speak. I didn't cry. I just listened and somehow, that was enough.

I attended the meetings for months, and eventually, for the first time in a long while, I felt like I was making progress. I was beginning to feel better, lighter, more present, and I knew the meetings had a lot to do with it. All this time, Guillermo and the kids had no idea I was going. I didn't want them to worry. I needed something that was just for me.

One day, I stood up and introduced myself for the first time. Angela looked over and gave me a nod of encouragement.

"Hello," I began, my voice trembling just slightly. "My name is Rosa Martinez. Earlier this year, my son was killed while serving on active duty. He had just become a father. He left behind a beautiful baby girl."

I paused, trying to steady my breath.

"As you can imagine, I was devastated. Even now, there are days when the grief is so heavy, I feel like I'm drowning. I didn't want to share this at first. I thought keeping it in made me strong. But I'm learning that sometimes, strength looks like saying it out loud."

One by one, the others in the room began thanking me for sharing. Their words were kind and sincere. For the first time in a long while, I felt like a weight had been lifted, not because the pain was gone, but because I wasn't carrying it alone anymore.

I was starting to feel better, and I truly believed Antonio wouldn't want me walking through life in sadness. Besides, I had to be strong for myself and for my family.

I invited Karime and Carolina over for dinner and finally confessed to them and Guillermo that I'd been attending grief support sessions. They were genuinely happy for me, relieved even. I also told them I was planning to retire in two years. After returning to work, I realized I just didn't have it in me anymore, not in the same way.

The girls had a lot of questions. Some I could answer. Others, I simply couldn't. And that was okay. For the first time, I felt like I didn't have to have it all figured out to be moving forward.

Carolina raised her glass. "You've earned it, Mami. I just hope you take time to rest and not fill every day with a to-do list."

Karime smiled. "You've spent your whole life taking care of us. Maybe now it's time to take care of yourself."

Guillermo reached for my hand under the table. "You know I support whatever brings you peace."

I nodded, swallowing back the lump in my throat. Their words wrapped around me like a warm shawl. For so long, I'd measured my worth by what I could give, what I could carry, what I could endure. Now, I was learning to receive.

After they left, I sat on the couch with the lights dimmed, the hum of the refrigerator the only sound in the house. I thought about what the next chapter might look like. Not just retirement, but renewal. The freedom to choose joy without guilt. The chance to spend slow mornings with my granddaughter. To travel. To breathe.

I wasn't done grieving, but I was beginning to imagine a life beyond the loss, and that, in itself, was a kind of grace.

Before going to bed, I walked into Antonio's old room. I hadn't been in there for a while, not for more than a minute or two. Tonight felt different. I opened the closet slowly, running my fingers across the shoulders of his old jackets, the scent of him still faint but familiar. I didn't cry. I didn't need to. I was past the storm, still healing, but no longer drowning.

I took down a small box from the top shelf. Inside were his baby shoes, a baseball cap he wore in high school, and a letter he once wrote me for Mother's Day. I carried it to the dining table and sat down. The words were messy, rushed, but full of love.

You always believed in me, even when I didn't believe in myself.

I folded the letter carefully and tucked it into a small photo album I planned to give to his daughter one day.

Then I turned off the lights, went upstairs, and let myself rest knowing that love, real love, doesn't end. It simply changes shape.

I lay beside Guillermo, and he wrapped his arms around me. We hadn't made love in a long time. Grief, distance, and the demands of life had created space between us. But that night, something shifted. He kissed me slowly, without rush, his hands exploring my body with the kind of tenderness that made me feel seen, desired, remembered.

He took his time, pleasuring me until I was breathless, until I found myself whispering his name and grabbing hold of him. When he did, nothing, not menopause, not MS, stood in the way. Our bodies moved in rhythm, like they were rediscovering each other. I turned over, settling into his favorite position. We both reached climax together, fully present, fully alive.

Afterward, we stayed close, our limbs tangled, skin still warm. Guillermo kissed me, and I rested my head on his chest, listening to the steady rhythm of his heartbeat. The room felt soft around us, wrapped in something sacred.

It wasn't just about lovemaking. It was about connection. About memory. About finding each other again after loss had hollowed out so much.

He kept me up late that night, loving me with a kind of gentle persistence that reminded me we were still here, still choosing each other. For the first time in a long while, I didn't feel broken. I felt whole. I felt like myself again.

"Babe, grandparents aren't supposed to be having sex," I teased, breathless.

"*¿Quién dijo?*"

We both laughed in a deep, joy-filled laughter that permeated through the room like music. The kind of laughter that heals.

Chapter 22

"Baila Yemaya"

Over the following years, our lives eased into a slower, more graceful rhythm. Intimacy looked different now, but it was no less tender. Guillermo and I would sit on the back porch, hands intertwined, sipping cold Maltas and reminiscing about the good old days. We still danced from time to time, sometimes to our favorite American love songs, other times to a little bachata when the mood struck.

We were now grandparents to ten beautiful children and two wonderful sons-in-law. Each grandchild was a joy in their own way. Rosa Alicia, the eldest, led the pack with her sharp wit, boundless curiosity, and natural confidence, already showing signs of becoming a boss in her own right. Watching them grow filled our lives with more purpose than we ever imagined. We took pride in knowing they were an extension of us, our stories living on in their laughter and light. Unlike us, they didn't have to carry the pain of the past, only the joy of the future. Any time we could spend with them and their parents felt complete.

We were preparing to host a Fourth of July picnic, the first gathering at our home since Antonio died. What better way to honor the birth of our nation than to be surrounded by family and friends? Everything had to be just right. Karime and Carolina took turns cleaning and organizing.

Antonio's childhood room had since become Rosa Alicia's when she visited. At twelve, she claimed it proudly. We made space for Lisa's other children from her current marriage as well. Though it would always be Antonio's room in spirit, it looked nothing like it once had. Guillermo painted it pink, and Karime used tracing stencils to paint fairies on the wall. Carolina and Karime bought bunk beds, a nightstand, a bookcase, bedding, and pillows. I framed the last photo I took of Antonio holding Rosa Alicia in the hospital delivery room, and placed it on the dresser.

The sun was blistering hot, casting a golden glow over the backyard as folding chairs were arranged in neat rows and the grill was fired up. The scent of marinated pork and sweet corn filled the air while a DJ mixed old-school salsa with just enough Stevie Wonder to keep things lively. Guillermo remained on the porch, directing the landscaper even as guests began arriving, using his cane like a conductor's baton to point out exactly how he wanted the lawn trimmed. Still the proud perfectionist after all these years.

"The lawn's good now," he said, wiping his brow with a handkerchief. "But I told him not to edge too close to my roses. He thinks because he's got a weed whacker, he's a damn landscaper." I laughed and handed him a cold coconut water. "It looks good, *viejo*."

We both knew he loved being involved. It gave him energy and purpose. This day gave us all a reason to celebrate everything we had built. Watching it unfold from our porch was enough for me. I looked around at the home we had scraped to buy, lived in, and loved and thought to myself: This is the dream. Maybe not the one we started with in Cuba, but the one we fought for every single day.

I moved throughout the kitchen, checking on the dishes one last time—potato salad, plátanos maduros, congri, pollo frito, hot dogs, hamburgers, and lechón asado. A four-layer white cake sat proudly on the counter, topped with blueberries and strawberries arranged like an American flag, next to Carolina's famous mango salad with shredded coconut on top. Karime was rinsing watermelon slices at the sink, singing softly to herself.

Carolina walked around like she was running a high-profile event, even putting her husband to work with last-minute store runs. "You'd think she was planning something for the White House," I whispered to Karime with a smirk.

"She gets it from you, Mami," Karime said, nudging me playfully. Carolina was a corporate event planner, and the White House was among her clients that existed in her Rolodex.

By noon, guests began to arrive. Carmen and Maya, Alberto, Isabelle, Angela, Yasmine, Pedro, neighbors, friends from church—all carrying foil-covered trays, folding chairs, and stories to share. The backyard was filled with laughter, the slap of dominoes on a folding table, and children running through sprinklers, squealing with delight. Parents sipped sodas and wine coolers, rum from plastic red cups, their conversations easy and full.

I stood at the edge of the porch with Guillermo, his arm wrapped tightly around my waist. From where we stood, I could see it all: our daughters moving through the crowd, the grandkids darting under tables, the grill piled high with ribs and corn, sizzling in the summer heat, and an American flag fluttering gently from the porch railing, catching the last light of the day.

The party lasted into the late evening. Fireworks cracked in the distance, reverberating through the neighborhood. The grandkids were bundled in lawn chairs, half-asleep under blankets, their faces sticky with barbecue sauce and popsicles.

Guillermo stayed on the porch for most of the evening, his cane resting beside him, a soft smile on his face. He played a few rounds of dominoes with Alberto and the neighbors, sharing jokes between hands. He looked tired, but it was the kind of tiredness that comes after joy.

When the last tray was wrapped in foil and the final guest had hugged their goodbyes, we made our way inside. Karime bathed and tucked the children into their sleeping bags, while Carolina loaded the dishwasher, humming something soft and familiar.

Upstairs, I helped Guillermo get bathed and changed into his pajamas. He moved slowly, more carefully than usual, and sat on the edge of the bed, scanning the room like he was taking stock.

"You okay?" I asked, running my hand along his back.

He nodded, eyes glassy. "I'm full, Rosa. Full in all the right ways."

We climbed into bed, and he took my hand like he always did, weaving his fingers through mine.

"*Buenas noches, mi amor*," he whispered.

"*Buenas noches*," I said, kissing the back of his hand. Then I turned off the light.

In the middle of the night, Guillermo found himself standing before the *Malecón*, the long seawall stretching beside Havana's coast like a winding path. The sky above him was stained with the warm amber of a fading Cuban sunset, casting long shadows across the cracked pavement. The waves crashed against the wall, while Yemeya blew a cool mist that kissed his face and drenched the linen of his guayabera.

Guillermo closed his eyes for a moment and let it wash over him. His bare feet felt the warmth of sunbaked stone beneath them, and everything around him felt both distant and deeply familiar.

Music drifted from an open window; an old Benny Moré tune, low and nostalgic. The sea air circled him like an embrace.

He took a breath, slow and steady, and opened his eyes to the Havana he once remembered: lines with clothes swaying between buildings, the distant clatter of dominoes, and a stray dog trotting through the streets.

He looked down and saw he was wearing his best white guayabera, the one I had gifted him for his birthday years ago. In the distance, a dance was underway. Lanterns swayed between trees, casting shadows that shone like candlelight. Women danced in their best dresses. Men clapped to the rhythm of the *clave.*

And then he saw me. The Rosita from my youth. My hair was long, black, full, loose and flowing. My laughter was infectious. I stood in the middle of the *Malecón*, waiting.

He walked toward me with his heart swelling with love. "May I have this dance?" he asked, extending his hand.

I accepted his hand, and my eyes sparkled. *"Claro que sí."*

And there, beneath a Cuban sky streaked with twilight, Guillermo danced. His body moved with a lightness he hadn't known in decades, his feet gliding over the worn stone. The music wrapped around him like warm air, each note lifting him higher and freer. He danced with joy in his heart and rhythm in his bones. Guillermo was a young man again, barefoot under the stars, dancing like his soul had just been set free.

The next morning, the house was still, except for the usual hum of the refrigerator and the soft creak of the floorboards.

I woke up first, stretching gently. Sunlight poured through the curtains, warm on my skin. I turned to Guillermo, his hand still holding mine.

"Caballero," I whispered. *"¿Quieres café?"*

He didn't answer.

His grip had loosened. Fingers slack, but still warm.

I sat up slowly. Something in my chest tightened, but there was no panic. I placed my other hand over his. "You went dancing, didn't you?"

A tear fell down my cheek, but my lips softened into a smile.

I didn't wake the girls, not right away. Instead, I stayed beside him, holding his hand as the morning light gently spilled into the room.

As dawn broke in Patterson, the sun was still setting in Havana, and in that golden light was Guillermo dancing his way home.

~The End ~

Epilogue

We buried Guillermo on a warm July morning, under a sky so blue that for a moment I thought we might be in heaven. We can't be, I reminded myself. Guillermo's not by my side.

The same flag that once waved proudly from our porch on holidays and homecomings now sat folded in my lap and would end up buried with Guillermo, a request he made years ago.

I will miss him grilling ribs in the backyard, embracing our grandchildren with an abundance of love, slapping down dominoes with a smirk on his face and a wink. It was hard to fathom that he was physically gone.

I felt his presence all over, even in the sway of the trees in our yard, in the scent of *café* brewing just before dawn. Most of all, I had comfort knowing Guillermo lived a full life, and well.

People said he looked peaceful, and he did. His face was relaxed, the lines softened as if time had surrendered its grip. I knew the truth they couldn't see. Guillermo had already gone home long before we gathered to say our goodbyes. His soul had moved on, gently and without fear, like it had always known the way.

So, I did the only thing that made sense to my heart. I wrote him a letter, a love letter to the man who held me through decades of joy and sorrow, who rode unscathed in storms with me and our children. A man who chose me every day, and let me choose him right back.

I tucked the love note into the pocket of his jacket before they closed the casket as my final gift. I whispered to him that I loved him. I also vowed that just because the page was turning, our story wasn't over.

Mi Amor,

You left so quietly, I almost didn't notice. One hand is still holding mine, as if to say, "Don't worry, I'm just stepping out for a bit."

I find myself setting out two cups of coffee in the morning, then smiling through the pain of losing you.

I miss the way you looked at our girls like they were made of gold. I miss how you used to touch my back when no one was looking. I even miss your long-winded stories about our days in *La Habana*.

But I know where you are. I saw it in your face that morning. You got to dance one last time, didn't you?

I'll be here a little longer, *Si Dios Quiere*, holding down the fort. But one day, I'll meet you in the *Malecón*. Save me a dance.

Un beso,

Rosita

Glossary of Key Terms

El papa de mi hijos: Spanish phrase meaning "the father of my children." Used by the narrator to refer to Guillermo.

Singao: A Cuban slang term, often used as an expletive expressing frustration or anger.

El paquetico: Spanish phrase meaning "the small package" or "the little pouch." Refers to the knitted pouch given to the narrator for safe passage.

Mi padrino: Spanish phrase meaning "my godfather." Refers to the narrator's godfather.

Yemayá: A major deity (*Orisha*) in the Yoruba religion, associated with the ocean, motherhood, and fertility.

Mi tía: Spanish phrase meaning "my aunt." Refers to the narrator's aunt in Miami.

Recuerda, mija: Spanish phrase meaning "Remember, my daughter." A term of endearment and advice used by a *tía*.

La azúcar y la presión: Spanish phrase meaning "sugar and pressure." Refers to diabetes and high blood pressure health conditions, which the narrator's *tía* warns are common in their family.

Barrio: Spanish word for "neighborhood," often referring to a working-class or traditional neighborhood.

Te amo, Rosita. No te olvides. Oijiste? Si, Guillermo: Spanish phrase meaning "I love you, Rosita. Don't forget. You hear? Yes, Guillermo." An exchange between Guillermo and the narrator.

Vamos a Nueva York: Spanish phrase meaning "Let's go to New York." Guillermo's surprise for the narrator.

¿Tú estás loco?: Spanish phrase meaning "Are you crazy?" The narrator's playful reaction to Guillermo's suggestion.

Novias: Spanish word for "girlfriends" or "sweethearts," specifically referring to women in a romantic relationship.

Bueno: Spanish word meaning "good" or "okay." Used here to express acceptance.

Ay, por favor: Spanish phrase meaning "Oh, please" or "Come on." Used to express disbelief or playful annoyance.

¿Quién es ella?: Spanish phrase meaning "Who is she?" The narrator's direct question to Guillermo about Sandra.

¿Cómo?: Spanish word meaning "How?" or "What?" Used here to express confusion.

Tu Voz: Spanish phrase meaning "Your Voice."

Tú no estás sola: Spanish phrase meaning "You are not alone." Reassurance given to the narrator.

Feminista: Spanish word for "feminist." Ms. Susan Roth's self-description.

Papi: Informal Spanish term for "Dad" or "Daddy." Used by the children to address Guillermo.

Qué lindo: Spanish phrase meaning "How beautiful" or "How lovely."

Coño: A Spanish expletive, used here to express admiration or desire.

La verdad: Spanish phrase meaning "The truth."

¿Por Qué Será?: Spanish phrase meaning "Why will it be?" or "Why is that?"

La crème de la crème: French phrase meaning "the best of the best." Used to describe Harvard University.

Mi amor: Spanish phrase meaning "my love." A term of endearment.

Saludo a elegua: Spanish phrase meaning "Salutation to *Elegua*." Eleguá (or Eleggua) is another Orisha in the Yoruba religion, the opener of roads and doors. The title suggests a new beginning or pathway.

Somos familia: Spanish phrase meaning "We are family."

Mija: Shortened form of *"mi hija,"* meaning "my daughter." A term of endearment.

Dios nos libre: Spanish phrase meaning "God save us" or "God forbid." Used humorously here.

La luz roja: Spanish phrase meaning "the red light." Refers to the red light bulb used by the narrator and Guillermo.

Malecón: The famous seawall promenade in Havana, Cuba.

Clave: A rhythmic pattern in Afro-Cuban music, often played on wooden sticks.

Sigue, Guillermo: Spanish phrase meaning "Continue, Guillermo" or "Go on, Guillermo."